HIDDEN GODDESS

MARINA FINLAYSON

FINESSE SOLUTIONS

Cover design by Karri Klawiter
Model stock image from Taria Reed/The Reed Files
Editing by Larks & Katydids
Formatting by Polgarus Studio

Published by Finesse Solutions Pty Ltd
2017/08/#01

Author's note: This book was written and produced in Australia and
uses British/Australian spelling conventions, such as "colour" instead
of "color", and "-ise" endings instead of "-ize" on words like "realise".

National Library of Australia Cataloguing-in-Publication entry:

Finlayson, Marina, author.
Hidden goddess / Marina Finlayson.
ISBN 9781925607000 (paperback)
Finlayson, Marina. Shadows of the Immortals; bk. 4.
Fantasy fiction.

For Mal, just because.

1

There's a fireshaper looking for you.

I put my beer down on the gleaming surface of the bar as Syl's voice sounded in my head. Harry, the bartender, continued the conversation Syl had interrupted, but I was no longer listening. My heart leapt, though my rational self knew it couldn't be Jake. We'd spent so much time together lately that I kept expecting to see him every time I turned around, but he was trapped in the underworld. I did my best to stop the little surge of emotion from crossing the mental link to Syl; she'd already told me I was acting like a love-struck teenager once today, and she didn't need any more ammunition.

A fireshaper was looking for me. Once, those words would have struck fear into my heart. There'd been a fireshaper looking for me for a long time, which was how Syl and I had ended up hiding out in sleepy Berkley's Bay in the first place. It had seemed like the last place a bigshot councillor like Erik Anders would think to search. But Anders had been dead for a couple of weeks now, and with the god Apollo taking an active interest in what his fireshapers got up to these days, a visit from a fireshaper was nowhere near as alarming as it used to be.

Anyone we know? It still paid to be cautious. It was hard to shake the habits of a lifetime. I'd started to see another side to fireshapers once I'd met Jake, but they weren't all like him.

That priest guy from the temple in Crosston.

Winston? The old Chinese one?

Yeah. Her mental voice was strong, as if she were close by. She was probably still sunning herself on the kitchen windowsill of our tiny apartment, just across the street from where I sat in the pub. We could only communicate this way when she was in her cat form—had she abandoned Winston on the doorstep to change forms?

Did you just leave him standing there while you shifted?

Nah. Didn't bother answering the door. It's so warm here and I'm too tired to get up.

Too lazy, you mean. Actually, she'd been out of bed before me, but there was no need to let truth get in the way of a good insult. *What if it had been Apollo? I'm sure he would have been thrilled to be left hanging on the doorstep because you couldn't be bothered to get off your furry butt.*

She snorted. *As if Apollo would have knocked anyway. He would have magicked the door open and waltzed in like he owned the place.*

She had a point there. *So if you didn't answer the door, how do you know he's looking for me?*

I can hear him talking to Joe and Holly. Our neighbours' door was right across the landing from ours. No doubt he'd knocked on it after being ignored by Syl. Cats could be such buttholes. *Want me to go out there and tell him where you are?*

If that wouldn't be too draining for you. Send him over to the pub.

I came back to my surroundings to find Harry staring expectantly at me. Damn, it must be my turn to say something. I took a gulp of beer to cover the awkward pause. The bar was more than half full, which was unusual for this time of day—too late for the lunch crowd and too early for the evening drinkers. The fine weather must have brought a few holiday-makers down from the city early. It was still spring, but by summer, Berkley's Bay would be awash in tourists.

A few of the locals at a table behind me were covering the same conversational ground as Harry and me: everyone had a theory about what had happened to Alberto, the vampire publican, who'd gone missing last week.

None of those theories, of course, accounted for the fact

that he wasn't a vampire at all, but a god: Hades, the Lord of the Underworld.

"Sorry, Harry, I missed that last bit."

"You look like you're half a world away, love." Harry rubbed at a non-existent spot on the bar. It was practically an antique, made of local wood, and the front of it was covered in intricate carvings of birds and wattle flowers. Alberto was very particular about keeping it polished to a high sheen, and had all his staff trained to wipe up spills straight away. Not using a coaster was practically a hanging offence. "Is everything all right?"

If only he knew. I was more than half a world away—my heart was in another plane altogether, along with a certain blue-eyed shaper who'd stolen it. Jake had agreed to spend a single night with the goddess of the River Styx in the underworld, in exchange for her help. Or so we'd thought. Of course, we'd all forgotten that, in the underworld, it was always night. The bitch had double-crossed us, leaving him trapped with her indefinitely, unless I could get help from a higher power. Even Apollo hadn't been able to force her to honour the spirit of her bargain rather than the letter.

Apollo thought only Hades or Zeus would be able to free Jake from Styx's clutches, which sucked big time, since both of them were missing. Zeus had been gone for ages, but Hades had only just disappeared, and I was far more worried about him than about the father of the gods. Hades was my friend, and not the kind of person to take off without warning. Besides, his bond with Cerberus, the great three-headed hellhound, had been broken two days ago, and that could only be bad news. Either the shadow shapers had caught him and collared him to stop him accessing his power, or he was dead. Not exactly a fabulous choice of options. I was worried sick about him.

"Everything's fine," I lied. "I'm just worried about Alberto."

"Aren't we all, darl?" The gold signet ring on Harry's little finger glittered in the light from the old-fashioned lamp overhead as he worked. Usually he wore a lot more jewellery to work. With his black uniform shirt, he looked like he was already in mourning for his missing employer. "I mean, I'm genuinely worried about him, and a man couldn't ask for a better boss—but we have to think of ourselves, too. What's going to happen to the pub if he never comes back? I'm paid up to the end of the month, and I'll work until then, but I can't keep going forever. A man's got to eat. I'll have to look for another job."

He'd probably have trouble finding one. Harry's track record wasn't the best. This job was the only one he'd managed to hang onto for more than a year, as he would happily tell anyone, as if his unreliability was a source of great pride.

"What will you do about the bookshop?" he asked.

Alberto the vampire was something of a real estate mogul in the area. As well as the pub, he owned several of the local businesses, plus half a dozen houses that he leased to the holiday crowd. Money was clearly no object when you were a god. He'd given me a job in the little second-hand bookshop when Syl and I had first come to town, plus cheap rent on the tiny apartment above it.

Today was Sunday, so the bookshop was closed, but what about tomorrow? With tourist season ramping up, I couldn't leave it closed, but there was no way I could go back to selling books with the fate of Jake and Hades hanging in the balance. If the shadow shapers had Hades, he would only live until they got their hands on his avatar. With that, they could kill him in such a way that all his power passed to them on his death. Our only hope was that he hadn't had it with him when he was caught.

I waved a vague hand. "Today's my day off, Harry. Don't make me think about work until tomorrow!"

He smiled, but worry still lurked in his eyes. He smoothed back his already sleek hair, gelled, as usual, within an inch of its life. Behind me, the door thudded closed, and his eyebrows rose in surprise.

"What?" I turned to see who'd come in and found Winston scanning the crowd. Most of the pub's patrons were staring straight back at him, their conversations momentarily silenced. Berkley's Bay might be in fireshaper territory, but that didn't mean that the order's priests were a common sight in the town. Apart from a statue to Poseidon down by the waterfront, there was very little attention paid to the official religion of the shapers in these parts. We didn't even have a shrine, much less a temple. Until Apollo himself had taken me to his great temple in Crosston, I'd never seen one of his priests, who rarely left the temple they served.

Winston wore the red robes that proclaimed he was on official business as a representative of the god, not the plainer white ones he'd had on last time I'd seen him … yesterday? Was it really only yesterday? It felt as though I'd lived three lifetimes in the last two weeks—so much had happened. The cuffs of his sleeves hung down nearly to his knees, heavy with embroidery, and perched on his thinning white hair was the most ridiculous red hat. Maybe it was supposed to be a sunburst, but it looked more like a tiny red octopus clinging to his head. No wonder the people in the bar stared.

Winston's expression cleared when he saw me, and he approached with a smile on his lined face. "Miss Lexi! There you are."

He settled himself on the bar stool next to me, arranging his robes carefully about him, moving with the deliberateness common to the elderly. A few wisps of white hair clung to his chin in the most pathetic excuse for a beard I'd ever seen.

"Can I get you something to drink, Reverence?" Harry asked.

"Water, thank you."

Harry moved away reluctantly, no doubt burning to find out what business one of Apollo's priests had with me. I was a little intrigued myself.

"I didn't expect to see you here, Reverence," I said. "You're a long way from home."

"I didn't expect to be here," he admitted, "but my lord desired that I find you. And please call me Winston, Miss Lexi. It's not right for someone like you to be calling me Reverence."

"Someone like me?" A sales assistant in a bookshop? A part-time thief? A woman who attracted trouble the way roadkill attracts flies?

"A companion of Lord Apollo." His voice was filled with awe. Yesterday, he'd met his god in person for the first time, which had to be a pretty full-on experience for someone who'd dedicated his life to the god's service.

"Trust me, it wasn't my idea to start hanging out with gods." Nor to lose my memory, or whatever the hell had happened to me. Nor to get on the fireshapers' Most Wanted list, and most especially not to fall for the most annoying fireshaper of all. The list of things I hadn't meant to do was long, and made for scary bedtime reading.

"But the gods have ideas for you. They have plans for us, Miss Lexi, and we must have faith in the paths of their choosing."

Yeah, right. The gods had withdrawn from the world so long ago that many people—including me, until a fortnight ago—didn't even believe in their existence. They were a story in a child's picture book, nothing more than a convenient fiction used by the shapers to justify their place at the top of the food chain. The idea that someone like Apollo gave a rat's arse what happened to anyone but his own gilded self was laughable.

However, there was no reason to burst Winston's adoring bubble. If he spent much time in Apollo's company, he'd work it out for himself soon enough.

"You know, every time you call me 'Miss Lexi', I age another five years. I tell you what—I'll call you Winston if you promise to call me Lexi. Deal?"

He beamed, nodding so vigorously I feared for the octopus's grip. There didn't seem to be anything but the power of prayer holding it on his head. "Deal."

Harry returned with a glass of water and set it on a coaster in front of the priest. Ice clinked as Winston took a long drink, a few drops escaping into his straggly beard.

"Have you had a long trip, Reverence?" Harry asked, digging for information as subtly as he could.

Winston laughed. "The longest I've had in many a year. I can't remember the last time I left the temple."

Another customer called Harry to the other end of the bar, and I grinned at the look of frustration on his face as he moved away again. I wondered if Winston had been vague on purpose.

"What *does* bring you here?" I asked.

"Lord Apollo has sent me to set up a temple."

"Whatever for?" How many temples did one god need? And why Winston? Surely there was some young flunky he could have sent, rather than uprooting an old man. Typical of Apollo. It wouldn't even have occurred to him that Winston might not be up to such exertion. The gods might be older than dirt, but they didn't have to deal with the trials of ageing the way humans did. Judging from the distortion of his knuckles and the way his hand shook as he raised the glass to his lips, I was guessing that Winston was pretty well acquainted with the pain of arthritis, at least.

"Lord Apollo foresees the need for travel between Crosston and Berkley's Bay in the coming weeks, and he would prefer if a faster option were available to him."

"I see." The gods could travel instantaneously between their own temples, and Berkley's Bay was a three-hour drive from the city. Of course Apollo would prefer the teleportation option. My irritation with him mellowed. At least he wasn't planning to abandon me now he had his powers back. I had the feeling I was going to need his help in the search for Hades. "Did you have a comfortable trip?"

"Very. One of the acolytes drove, and I snoozed in the back seat." He winked at me. "At my age, one must never pass up the opportunity for a nap."

I hid a yawn behind my hand, still exhausted from recent events. "That's good advice at any age. You must be pretty important to have your own driver." I didn't want to admit how ignorant I was about the priesthood—he could be the high priest, for all I knew.

He smiled. "Not important at all. My fireshaping was never strong enough to rise above the level of priest—I just don't have a licence. I always wanted to learn, but somehow, there never seemed to be enough time. Or perhaps my superiors decided I didn't have the temperament to make a good driver. I was sometimes impatient with temple life when I was a young acolyte."

Looking at him now, that was hard to imagine. He sat very still, his gnarled hands folded neatly on the bar, and projected an air of serenity.

"Have you served the temple all your life?"

"Since I was seven years old. And never in all that time did I expect to meet my lord face to face." He beamed, his eyes nearly disappearing into the wrinkles around them. "These are strange and wonderful times we are living in, Lexi."

"You can say that again." Although maybe a bit heavier on the *strange* than the *wonderful*.

"Lord Apollo wished me to speak with you about facilitating the purchase of a house in the central part of town, which could be converted to a temporary temple."

I was relieved that Apollo didn't expect some grand edifice to be erected on short notice. "I'm surprised he didn't tell you to speak to the mayor about it."

The mayor was a watershaper, and not one of my favourite people, but he was the local representative of the shapers. I would have expected shaper business to be routed through him, particularly something as big as establishing a temple.

"He said he would prefer the existence of the temple to remain private for now."

Ah. Okay, that put a different slant on it. I took in the glory of his red robes, topped off with the bizarre octopus hat. "You know, you're not exactly travelling incognito. People will wonder what a temple priest is doing in a place like this. You don't look like you're on vacation. There'll be talk, and rumours."

"That is true." He looked crestfallen. The poor guy probably didn't even own any regular clothes. "I didn't consider this in my rush to do my lord's bidding."

I managed not to roll my eyes, and took a sip of beer. Winston brooded for a moment before his face cleared.

"We will tell everyone that I am your uncle and I am here to visit you."

Beer sprayed everywhere. Coughing, I snagged a serviette from further down the bar and wiped it up as Winston watched me anxiously. Yes, I was sure people would believe Winston was my uncle. My Chinese uncle.

"Winston, we don't look anything alike. You'll have to think of something else."

But it seemed he was too taken with the idea to let it go. "Perhaps you were adopted! Or I could be." I shook my head. "An old family friend, then. An honorary uncle."

I took a deep breath. "Let's just focus on getting you a house first. I have a friend who can help with that—she's just started a job as a real estate agent. She should be here soon."

"Really?" He beamed in satisfaction. "How fortunate! You see, Lexi, if we have faith, the gods will provide."

"It's nothing to do with the gods. She agreed to meet me here long before you arrived," I said, unable to keep a note of irritation from creeping into my voice. "That's why I'm sitting here. Waiting for her."

"Trust in the path," he said, ignoring everything I'd just said.

I drained the last of my beer, seething. If the gods were capable of arranging paths for their supplicants, why the hell couldn't they predict their own futures? If they were so all-seeing, how come they were getting killed off left, right, and centre?

I wasn't buying it. If Apollo had the kind of power that Winston was claiming, he would never have spent a year as a prisoner with a collar around his neck. He wouldn't now be trying to set up a new temple so he could sneak around without being traced. Divine power clearly had its limitations. From what I'd seen, the gods were too busy living their own lives to care about anyone else's.

2

Rosie arrived a few minutes later, rushing in in a cloud of perfume and breathless apologies. "Sorry I'm late. Got held up with a client who wanted to examine every last cupboard in the house I was showing." Her eyes slid sideways as she kissed me, checking out my peculiar drinking buddy.

"It's fine. I wasn't going anywhere. Rosie, this is my … ah … friend, Winston." To Winston, I said: "Rosie is the real estate agent I was telling you about."

"A pleasure to meet you, my dear," Winston said, with a strange little nod that looked like it wanted to be a bow but thought better of it.

Rosie slid onto the stool on the priest's other side, her professional curiosity aroused. I hadn't seen her since she'd taken this job, but she certainly looked the part in a navy business suit, her light brown hair tied back in a neat ponytail. "Are you in the market for a home, Winston?"

"Not a home, precisely." Winston licked his lips nervously, giving me an uneasy glance. Did he have a problem lying? How quaint! And so strange for a fireshaper. "More of a, um, holiday house." His expression brightened as inspiration dawned. "Yes! A holiday house for retired priests."

"Well, I can certainly help with that." Rosie fished her business card out of her purse and handed it to him. "Come and see me tomorrow and I can show you a few places. What kind of house are you looking for?"

Winston glanced down at the card. "Let's talk about it tomorrow. I don't wish to interrupt your time with your friend with business." He slid off his stool, looking like a man with places to be. Nice exit. Very smooth. He could spend the rest of the evening dreaming up requirements for his imaginary holiday house.

"Do you have somewhere to stay tonight?" I asked.

"My acolyte has booked us into the Goodnite Motel. Hopefully, the comfort there will be better than the spelling." He smiled at us both. "Good afternoon, ladies."

"Bye."

When he was gone, Rosie regarded me with raised eyebrows. "Where on earth did you meet him?"

"We have a mutual friend. In Crosston."

She shook her head. "You do know some odd people."

Ha! She didn't know the half of it. "Can I get you a drink? How are you? How's the new job working out?"

She signalled to Harry, and ordered a white wine. "Busy. We really need another agent, but Gerard's too tight to put anyone else on. And I'm the new girl so I can't really say anything. I'm still learning the ropes."

Harry delivered her wine, and she took a grateful sip. She looked tired, which wasn't unusual, but a few wisps of hair had escaped her ponytail and there was a smudge of something—lunch?—on the collar of her jacket, as if she hadn't had a moment to stop all day. Sunday was a busy day for real estate agents.

"How's Cody?" I asked. Her face brightened, as it always did when she talked about her son. He was a bright, chatty kid who loved reading, and he'd often visited me in the bookshop after school. He mainly lived with Rosie, but he stayed over with Joe and Holly one night a week, or sometimes two. "What does he think of his new little half-sister?"

"I think he's looking forward to when she gets a bit older. He says all she does is sleep."

"Is he okay with the fact that she's a werewolf and he's not?"

Rosie grimaced. "I don't know. He hasn't mentioned it, and I don't want to bring it up and *make* him think about it if it hasn't occurred to him yet." Rosie was human, which meant that her son with Joe was human, too, but since Holly was a werewolf herself, Joe's daughter with his second wife was a full werewolf. "Anyway, there's nothing anyone can do about it, so he'll just have to live with it. He's been too busy keeping on my good side lately to have much time for anything else. He's been texting me every day at work to tell me when he's home from school."

She laughed, and I joined in. Cody had given us all a scare when he'd disappeared with a friend one day after school recently. There'd been a whole search party out combing the bush for him. His mother had been overjoyed to get him back safe and sound, but I could well believe the apron strings had tightened since then. Cody would be working hard to convince Rosie that he was trustworthy again.

That was the night I'd met Jake.

"You look tired," Rosie said.

"Yeah, it's been a busy couple of weeks." She raised her eyebrows again, and I shrugged. "Long story."

The story had begun that night in the wet bush, when Jake and I had rescued Cody, and it was still going on. I just hoped there was a happy ending in store. I missed Jake more than I would have thought possible, considering the short length of time I'd known him. But the kind of trials we'd been through together had a way of creating an instant intimacy. I'd seen sides of Jake's personality that I was willing to bet few people knew existed—and I liked what I saw.

"So, you said you wanted to talk to me about something?"

"Yeah. Joe said you were practically the last person to see Alberto before he disappeared." Sometimes I had trouble remembering to say "Alberto" instead of "Hades". "I was hoping you might be able to give me a clue as to why he vanished."

She shook her head. "I'm just as mystified as everyone else. We only chatted for a minute. Nothing seemed unusual."

"What did you talk about?"

"Just everyday things."

She took a sip of her wine and I closed my eyes for a moment, trying to control my impatience. This was not just some vampire wandering off. She had no idea what was at stake here. "Like what?"

"He was just asking me how Cody was. He was nice like that, always interested in everyone. I told him Cody was worming his way back into my good books and he laughed. Then I mentioned Cody's new teacher." She shrugged. "Nothing, really."

"That was it?" Damn, I'd been hoping for something more.

She twirled the end of her ponytail around her finger, thinking. "Pretty sure. He left right after that."

Was it something she'd said? "What were your exact words, can you remember?" I was clutching at straws, but I didn't have any other leads. My helplessness galled me. I should be out there *fixing* this—finding Hades, saving

Jake—and instead, I was stuck here, flailing around in the dark.

She shrugged again. "I just said it was a shame that Becky had left so suddenly, because Cody was really happy in her class, but the new teacher seemed to be working out okay."

"And what did he say?"

"He asked when Becky had left. I thought he knew, because everyone had been talking about it, and you know how he likes to gossip when he's minding the bar."

"What was the big deal with Becky leaving?" I'd never really warmed to Becky, though Holly had liked her well enough. She'd always struck me as looking down her nose at the people around her, particularly the shifters, though she acted as sweet as sugar to their faces.

"It was just so sudden. One day, Cody comes home from school and says Miss Campbell never turned up that morning. People were worried at first, frightened that something bad had happened to her. The police even went around to her house looking for her, but she'd packed up all her clothes and personal items and taken off. Just like that. Never said a word to anyone. Old Mr Lee said he'd seen her drive past his place that morning, her car all loaded up like she was going on a holiday. Can you believe that? How could she just walk out on her job like that?"

It was pretty weird. "And when was this?"

"The day after that car accident at the pub, the one that wrecked the doors. Remember?"

Trust me, I wasn't likely to forget that "car accident" any time soon. I would have died that day, and Jake and Holly, too, if Alberto hadn't blown the doors off the pub and come to our rescue. He'd blown the lid on his real identity at the same time, though he'd wiped the fact that he was Hades from the memories of everyone who'd seen his true self, except for Jake and me.

But Becky hadn't been there, so why would the fact that she'd skipped town the day after have bothered Hades?

"What was his reaction when you told him about Becky leaving?"

"Nothing much. You know what he's like—it's practically impossible to tell what he's thinking sometimes."

"Did he say anything else?"

"Just 'goodbye, it was nice chatting', or something like that. Then he left."

I couldn't figure it out. Did he think Becky had been working with Erik Anders? That didn't seem likely, since she'd been living in Berkley's Bay for at least a couple of years. And why would it matter anyway, if the traitorous councillor was dead?

Perhaps he thought she was a mole. She'd always struck me as a secret One Worlder. Once, I'd thought that that human organisation was the worst threat out there, just because they thought the world would be a better place without shapers or shifters in it. They made plenty of noise about it, but rarely took any action. Of course, that was before I had discovered the shadow shapers existed, with their plans to destroy all the gods by stealing their powers for themselves. If she was a mole for the shadow shapers, it would definitely be a problem, but I just couldn't see the connection. She hadn't seen the fight outside the pub, so leaving right after it must be coincidence. Hades must have seen something else significant about her abrupt departure. But what?

My phone buzzed in my pocket, signalling a text coming in. I didn't recognise the number. It only said "Hes", as if someone had started typing "He's", then realised they had the wrong number and given up. I shrugged and put the phone away.

Rosie patted my hand reassuringly. "I wouldn't worry about him too much—I'm sure he'll turn up sooner or later. He's a vampire. There's not much that could take him down."

I smiled, but said nothing. Actually, he was a god, which meant he was vulnerable, since no one knew how the shadow shapers were catching them. Every god they'd captured, whether they survived the experience or not, came away with a hole in their memory where the "who" and "how" should have been. That was why Apollo was so jumpy about people knowing his whereabouts. Since he couldn't remember how he'd been snared the first time, there was no way to guard against it.

"Hey, there!" said a familiar voice. "Mind if we join you?"

Syl stood there, grinning, her dark hair in its customary long braid over one shoulder, Lucas looming behind her like a gigantic shadow. He was a good head-and-a-half taller than the diminutive cat shifter, and built like a brick shit house.

Rosie finished her wine and slid off her stool. "Lucas! I haven't seen you in ages." She stretched up to give her ex-brother-in-law a kiss on his stubbly cheek. "When did you get into town?"

"Last night." The big werewolf gave her a crushing hug.

"Make sure you drop in for a proper visit before you leave." She scooped her handbag off the bar. "I'm sorry, I've got to run now—I told Cody I'd be home by four. See you later, Lexi." She smiled politely at Syl and hurried away.

Syl stared after her, a comical expression of surprise on her face. "She didn't recognise me."

"No kidding, genius. She's never see you in human form before."

"I know, it's just … weird." She claimed Rosie's stool and sighed. "Maybe I have spent too long as a cat." She shot me a sidelong look, her green eyes stern. "No need to say I told you so."

"Wouldn't dream of it."

Lucas went off to buy a round of drinks and a smile curved the corners of her mouth as she watched him. "There are a few things I've missed about being human."

I followed the direction of her gaze. The hunky werewolf was certainly a tempting package, fit and strong-looking. He was a taller version of Joe, with the same brown eyes, and hair that tried to curl if it wasn't cut often enough. If I hadn't been so interested in a certain fireshaper, I might have made Joe's dreams come true by hooking up with his brother. "Like what? Drinking beer?"

She grinned, a wicked glint in her eye. "That too."

I went home from the pub about nine o'clock. Syl laughed and said I had no stamina, but the truth was, I was still exhausted. I fell into bed and barely had time to pull the blankets up before I fell asleep.

Voices woke me much, much later, speaking in those peculiarly carrying tones that slightly tipsy people always used when they were trying to be quiet. Lucas's deep rumble sounded just outside my door, then Syl's unmistakeable giggle. Wow, it had been a long time since I'd heard that. Obviously they'd had a good evening after I'd left. Maybe I'd been wrong about her fancying Apollo. She certainly hadn't wasted any time hooking up with Lucas. I smiled into the darkness and rolled over.

Syl's door closed, but I still heard the creak of protest from her bed as they got into it. How on earth were the two of them going to fit into her narrow single bed? There'd be bits of Lucas hanging out all over the place. I heard more giggling, soon followed by some other sounds. Gah. I pulled the pillow over my head to block the noises. These walls were thinner than I'd realised.

Bright daylight glowed around the edges of the blind when I woke again. There were no signs of life from Syl's room. I grinned to myself as I crept past her closed door. After the night they'd had, they probably wouldn't be surfacing until late. Later—it was nearly ten already.

I grabbed a juice from the fridge and stood looking out the kitchen window at the street below while I drank it. Maybe I'd treat myself to breakfast at the café opposite, then go check on the bookshop. I had to decide what to do about it—I didn't really want to leave it closed, but I couldn't see myself working there again for a while. Maybe not ever, which made me sad. Life had been so much simpler when I was a bookshop employee—filled with the smell of old books, chats with customers, and the satisfaction of keeping everything neat and orderly. Admittedly, I'd had the fear of being found by a fireshaper who wanted to kill me hanging over my head, but otherwise, it had been a pretty good life.

There were only a few other customers in the café, and

I took a seat with my back to the wall, looking out at the street. Old habits died hard, though no one was hunting me anymore. I ordered a big breakfast, surprised by how hungry I felt. I guess sleep wasn't the only thing I'd missed out on lately. There'd been a few skipped meals, too.

By the time I'd worked my way through the heaped plate of bacon, eggs, tomato, and mushrooms that arrived, a small black cat had appeared on my kitchen windowsill across the street.

I didn't expect to see you up for hours yet, I said. *You had a pretty big night.*

Sooo big. Her mental voice purred with self-satisfaction.

Where's Lucas?

Still asleep. I think I broke him.

I smothered a laugh, and wiped the last of the bacon grease from my mouth with the tiny paper serviette. *Doesn't he have to get back to Crosston to go to work?* His boss was probably still cranky with him for skipping out on work the other night to drive me to Berkley's Bay.

He said he's going to take special leave.

Special leave? What for?

The little black cat licked a paw delicately, almost languorously. *I'm special, so he's taking leave.*

Just be careful you don't get your heart broken. He's a bit of a ladies' man, according to Joe. That was one reason Joe had been so keen to match me up with his brother—he thought I'd be a steadying influence. Ha! He didn't know me nearly as well as he thought he did.

I can handle him. Don't worry about me—I'm not looking for a 'happily ever after' here.

Just a 'sexually sated for now'?

Something like that.

Sounded like he was meeting your criteria last night.

He most certainly was. Who said cats and dogs can't play nicely together?

I snorted. *Don't let him catch you calling him a dog.* Werewolves got particularly sensitive about that.

I waved to her as I came out of the café, and she yawned ostentatiously. Maybe someone should have got more sleep last night. But if her lost sleep and its cause made her this chipper, I was all for it. This cocky Syl who drank and flirted in human form, who could go all night and still be up the next morning delicately grooming herself as the smuggest cat in creation—this was the Syl I'd been missing. It was good to see her again. I was inclined to approve of her new best friend, even if he was louder in the sack than I would have preferred. If he hung around for long, I'd have to invest in some earplugs to wear to bed.

As I crossed the street towards the bookshop, a man came out of Tegan's hair salon next door sporting a neatly trimmed white beard. It wasn't until he smiled at me that I realised it was Winston.

I stopped on the pavement, taking in the new, shorter haircut, the grey trousers with the neat crease pressed into them, and the pale green shirt. "Wow, look at you! I didn't recognise you."

He looked down at his shiny new shoes self-consciously. "I thought I should look less conspicuous when I go out today with Rosie looking at houses. You were right about how much my temple robes made me stand out." He sighed. "I'm afraid I've never been much good at subterfuge."

"That's not actually a bad thing," I pointed out. "But no one would ever guess now that you're a priest."

He beamed. "The tiger lady told me where to go to get the clothes, and what to buy. She's been very helpful."

That figured. Tegan loved organising other people. "And she cut your hair, too. You've had a busy morning."

He gestured back at the hair salon. "I was just showing her what I'd bought."

Tegan waved to us through the window. I bet he'd been under instructions to come back for inspection, so she could make sure his choices were up to her standards. It was a wonder she hadn't insisted on going shopping with him, too. Probably only the fact that the salon was crammed with people this morning saved him, otherwise she would have. Winston nodded gravely at her. Perhaps waving was beneath the dignity of a priest. She gave him a cheerful thumbs up before she went back to cutting hair.

He walked a few paces with me before I stopped at the bookshop door and pulled out my keys.

"I'm going in here. This is where I work."

Winston looked up at the windows of my apartment, and nodded approvingly. "That's very convenient. Is that your cat? She has a good view from up there—she can see the whole street."

I paused, my hand halfway to the door. The keys jingled once then fell still. "It's Syl, actually. She's a cat shifter." *She has a good view from up there.* My heart began to beat a little faster.

I turned and looked up and down the street with new eyes. *She can see the whole street.* The other shops were like the bookshop—they all had rooms of some kind above them. There was an accountant's office over the café across the road. Tegan had a yoga studio above her salon. The pub had accommodation for travellers in its upstairs rooms. Others used their upstairs rooms as additional storage for the businesses below, and a couple were apartments like ours. All of them had windows that overlooked the street, giving anyone looking out a good view of what was happening below.

What if Becky had been looking out of one of those windows when the shit with Anders went down? I cast my mind back, trying to picture the street—but it was useless. I'd been far too occupied with the fireballs flying back and forth, and the threat of impending death, to pay any attention to what was happening above our heads.

Would Hades have noticed her? He said he'd wiped the memory of the battle from the minds of everyone who'd seen, but what if he'd missed one? People would have rushed to their windows as soon as they heard the noise of the crash, but if Becky was a mole for the shadow shapers, she would have taken extra care not to be seen, once she realised what she was witnessing. It would have been a dream come true for her, to find the Lord of the Underworld announcing his identity on the open street.

And next morning, she would have packed up her life in Berkley's Bay and hurried back to her masters to report what she'd discovered. Maybe that night in the pub with Rosie, hearing about the sudden inexplicable departure of one of the local schoolteachers, Hades had realised his mistake. But why hadn't he sought refuge in the underworld when he realised his cover was blown? No shadow shaper could reach him there. So where had he gone?

"Yes," I said, glancing up at Syl, "she does. A really good view."

"I must go," Winston said. "Your friend Rosie is picking me up at eleven."

"Good luck with the house hunting."

And when she'd reported Hades' whereabouts to her

masters, what had they done? Whatever they usually did when they found a god, I supposed. It always seemed to work, whatever their method was. Gods disappeared and, if the shadow shapers got their hands on their avatars, gods died. Wherever he'd gone, they'd found him, and the best I could hope for was that he was indeed a captive. Because if he wasn't, he must already be dead.

3

Little Mireille was crying as I came up the stairs to the apartment. Her newborn wail sounded more like a kitten crying than a human, though Joe assured me that in a couple of months she'd be much louder. He'd been through it all before with Cody.

Holly was a first-time mum, but she was a pretty laid-back person, and motherhood hadn't changed that. "Come in, it's open!" she called when I knocked, so I let myself into the tiny apartment, a mirror image of our own. In a moment, she appeared, Mireille over her shoulder. She was rubbing the baby's back with firm strokes.

"How are you doing?" I asked.

"We're fine, aren't we, Miri?" She kissed the top of the downy little head, ignoring the noise. A small towel was draped over her shoulder. "Just need to get a burp out."

"Do you need anything?" How could she appear so calm with the baby wailing in her ear like that?

"More sleep." She did look tired. Her brown hair was pulled up into a messy knot on the top of her head, and there were dark circles under her eyes. She was a tiny thing, even more delicate than Syl; it was hard to believe she could turn into a werewolf. But appearances were deceptive—she was small, but tough. Even though she only came up to Joe's shoulder, there was no doubt who was the dominant partner in their marriage. "Always need more sleep. But everything else is under control—everyone's been so helpful. Have a seat."

I sat down, but she continued to pace, jiggling the baby as she patted her tiny back.

"Norma's been bringing meals every day, which is very sweet, but now we have enough food here to feed an army. And it's not as though I can't cook—I'm not an invalid, I just had a baby. Women have been doing it for centuries."

Most of them hadn't had such a traumatic birth experience as Holly had, but I didn't bring that up. I could understand why Norma might be overcompensating.

Holly's efforts suddenly bore fruit as Mireille burped, and I discovered what the towel was for as a rush of partly digested milk came with the burp. Already expert, Holly wiped it all up with the towel, dumped the towel in the bathroom, then came to sit down with a baby who was now magically quiet in her arms.

"That's typical pack behaviour, though, isn't it, for everyone to rally around?" I asked. Holly's parents-in-law were the alphas of the local pack. "You could hardly expect Norma not to get a little excited when it's her own granddaughter."

Holly rolled her eyes. "This child already has more toys than I can fit in her toy basket, and she's only two weeks old. Don't you, darling? Grandma is spoiling you!"

Mireille gazed up at her, drawn to the sound of her mother's voice, and Holly and I both stared at her for a long moment. There was something so compelling about babies. Such tiny perfection. As I watched, her eyes began to drift closed, and Holly sighed.

"She doesn't stay awake long. I suppose I should enjoy it while it lasts, but I kind of wish I had something to do while she slept."

"Don't you sleep yourself?" It seemed like the ideal way to catch up on all that lost sleep.

"I can't sleep in the daytime, unfortunately. Never have been able to. This place is so small it doesn't take much effort to keep it tidy, which leaves me with a lot of time on my hands. There's only so much daytime TV a girl can stomach. I'd love to get out and see people, but she sleeps so much, and I don't want to drag her all over town." She smiled at me. "Anyway, it's good to see you—it's nice to have someone to talk to. What's happening?"

"I was just wondering if you knew where Becky lived." She'd been a friend of Holly's—or, at least, Holly had been a friend of hers. Who knew whether Becky had really liked her shifter "friends" or if that had been part of her charade. I'd last seen her at Holly's baby shower.

"Becky Campbell? In Cranston Street. Tiny house with a big jacaranda in the front yard. Why?"

"It's starting to look as though she had something to do with Hades' disappearance."

"Seriously? She was a primary school teacher. And a human." Shifters had a hard time seeing humans as any kind of threat.

"I think she was secretly working with the shadow shapers. I'd like to have a look at her house, see if she left any hints behind in her rush to get out of town."

Holly looked doubtful. To be honest, I was doubtful myself. I wasn't expecting to find a signed confession, or a map of their hideout or anything, but I didn't know what else to do. "The police already looked at her place."

"Yeah, but it wasn't a crime scene. They didn't go over it with a fine-tooth comb, they were just looking for her, making sure she wasn't dead on the floor or anything. Rosie told me all her personal stuff was gone, so they were satisfied that she was just skipping out on her landlord and left it at that."

"If all her personal stuff is gone, what are you hoping to find?"

"I don't know." I hated feeling helpless. "But I figure it won't hurt to look. There could be something."

The door opened and Lucas wandered in, his rumpled hair and bleary eyes making it obvious he'd just crawled out of bed. "You guys have no food in your fridge," he said to me in a plaintive tone, as if I'd emptied the fridge just to torture him.

"There's plenty in ours," Holly said. "Your mother's been going crazy."

He helped himself to a hunk of cold steak and stood in the middle of the kitchen wolfing it down. Eww. Cold steak—and it was practically raw in the middle. As soon as it was gone, he grabbed half a lasagne and a spoon, and came and plonked himself down on the end of the couch.

"Heard you talking," he said. "You planning on breaking in?"

I grinned. I liked the casual way he said it, as if breaking in somewhere was no big deal. "Just for a quick look."

"I'll come with you."

I indicated the enormous bulk of him, sprawled on the lounge. "You're great for breaking down doors, but kind of conspicuous for more subtle work."

He gave me a wounded look. "I can do inconspicuous. What if you need back-up?"

"It's just a little break and enter, and a quick look around. I won't need back-up."

"If you want to be quick, it would be faster with more than one person," he said through a mouthful of lasagne. His hair stuck up like a rooster's comb at the back. "It'll take longer to search the whole house by yourself."

"And you probably need a lookout," Syl added from the doorway. She came in and perched herself next to him, on the arm of the lounge, snagging a scrap of lasagne from his dish and popping it delicately into her mouth. "I can help with that."

I rolled my eyes. "Guys, burglary is not a team sport. I'd be better off on my own."

Syl frowned at me as she tried to smooth Lucas's hair into shape. "I thought you'd gotten over that god complex of yours. You don't have to do everything on your own. We're your friends. Helping each other is what friends do."

She seemed to think that ended the discussion. When even Holly agreed it was a good idea, I gave up arguing. It should be simple enough.

The house in Cranston Street was as tiny as Holly had said. Painted a cheerful yellow, it was almost hidden behind overgrown shrubs and dwarfed by the majestic jacaranda that dominated the front yard. The garden beds were full of onion weed. Clearly, Becky had been no gardener. A For Sale sign on the front lawn said that this renovator's dream offered two good-sized bedrooms and a sunny, north-facing backyard. Not a lot to recommend it. Hopefully the rent had been cheap, at least.

There was no one on the street as Lucas and I left Syl in position on the low brick wall at the front of the property, ready to alert us if anyone appeared. She sat washing her little black paws in the sun as we walked up the driveway and around to the back of the house. A couple of pots on the small back porch held wilted plants. I checked under them in case someone had left a spare key, as people often did, but came up empty-handed.

Oh, well, on to Plan B.

"You always carry a set of lock picks with you?" Lucas asked as I crouched down and got to work on the back door.

"No, just special occasions."

He watched me work for a moment, then wandered off to try all the windows along the back of the house.

Your new boyfriend is taking to the criminal life like a natural, I told Syl. *Norma would be horrified if she knew.*

Rubbish. She thinks the sun shines out of his arse. He could rob a bank in front of her and she wouldn't blink.

Nothing moving out there? My patient jiggling was rewarded with a click. *We're going in.*

It's all clear. Be careful.

Of what? It wasn't as if Becky would have booby-trapped her rental house. With Lucas at my shoulder, I stepped inside. Though it was the middle of the day, all the blinds were drawn, so it was gloomy. We were in a small kitchen, with cupboards above and below the work area. I opened the closest one and found a neat stack of crockery. Becky must have been in a hurry to skip town.

I moved the plates to one side and checked all around them. Lucas started on the cupboards below the sink.

"What exactly are we looking for?" he asked.

"I don't know. Anything that might give us a clue where she came from, or where she might have gone. Letters, ticket stubs … I don't know. Something."

ID from one of the human cities would have been nice. It was probably a wild goose chase, but it was better than sitting around waiting for Apollo. He could be busy sorting out the fireshapers for days, even weeks, and I couldn't bear to do nothing in the meantime. Every moment that passed was another moment that Jake was forced to spend in Styx's hands; another moment that Hades languished in captivity, cut off from his power.

We soon finished in the kitchen and moved through to the first bedroom. It was tiny and completely empty—there wasn't even a bed. I could only tell it was meant to be a bedroom because it had a small cupboard built in, with three shelves and a hanging space for clothes.

The other bedroom was bigger, and contained a double

bed. The wardrobe there was bigger, too, with sliding mirrored doors. Lucas slid the right-hand door out of the way, revealing white drawers and shelves built in. He pulled each drawer open, revealing that they were all empty.

"Check the undersides of them, too," I said.

Found anything yet? Syl asked.

Nope. Lucas's eyes gleamed as he pulled out each drawer completely and turned them over. He was clearly enjoying himself. *Lucas is having a great time checking for secret compartments.* The bottom drawer stuck and refused to come all the way out. *Ooh, hang on, he might have found something.*

A secret compartment? That's awesome!

"Don't break it," I cautioned Lucas.

He tugged more gently, and wiggled the drawer on its runners. After a moment, he succeeded in lifting the drawer free, revealing a pair of black socks and a whole bunch of fluff and dust beneath it. He turned the drawer over with a crestfallen look. There was nothing odd about the bottom of it. It had just been caught on the socks. They'd probably slipped out the back of an overfull drawer and ended up trapped on the floor below it. He checked inside each sock, just in case, but there was nothing in them.

"Damn," said Syl. She lounged against the doorframe, arms folded. "I wanted to see a secret compartment."

"I thought you were watching the street in case we got company?"

"It's dead as a dodo out there. No one's going to come."

We moved into the lounge room next, where the TV stood on top of an entertainment unit with three drawers. None of them held a thing, and the small bookcase was empty, too. Syl got down on the floor to look under the two lounges, then sat back on her heels. "There might be something in the bathroom."

I doubted it. Despite her hurry to leave, Becky had been careful to remove all traces of her life from this place. Furniture and kitchen utensils left no clue that I could follow.

"I could check that shed in the back yard, too," Lucas offered. Before I could reply, his head whipped around to stare at the front door. "Shit. We've got company."

He moved back into the kitchen as a key turned in the lock. Syl disappeared, leaving a black cat streaking for cover under the lounge, but I wasn't quick enough. The door opened, revealing a very surprised Rosie on the doorstep.

"Lexi? What on earth are you doing? How did you get in here?" Frowning, she stepped inside, followed by Winston, still resplendent in his new clothes. She was showing him *this* house? I could have kicked myself. I was losing my touch—I'd managed to steal the ring off the Ruby Adept's finger without getting caught, and now this? It was downright embarrassing. Why hadn't I borrowed the eyes of some of the local birds to keep watch for me, instead of relying on Syl? Curiosity may not have killed the cat, but it had sure landed me in an awkward situation.

"Oh, hi, Rosie. Hi, Winston." My brain spun as I tried to come up with some kind of excuse. The look of shock and disapproval on Rosie's face was making it hard to think. Out of the corner of my eye, I could see the end of a black tail under the lounge. Lucas, of course, was nowhere to be seen. He'd moved surprisingly fast for such a big guy. *Thanks for your help, guys.* "I was just, ah …" The tail twitched as the moment lengthened. "Just looking for a cat."

"Looking for a *cat*?" Rosie's tone was heavy with disbelief as she frowned at me. Now I knew how Cody must feel when he got into trouble. "What are you talking about?"

Zeus's balls. *Come on, dammit, you can do this.* "I was out walking with Lucas. It's such a nice day for a walk, isn't it? And as we went past here, we thought we heard a kitten miaowing. I knew Becky had moved out, so we had a look in the windows, and it wasn't a kitten, but there was a little black cat in here. We figured it was stuck inside, so we came in to help. To get it out."

"I can't see it anywhere," Lucas called from the kitchen, then did a reasonably convincing double take as he came back into the room and saw Rosie and Winston. "Oh, hi. I didn't realise we had company. Nice to see you again, Rosie."

Her frown only deepened at the sight of her ex-brother-in-law. "What cat? How would a cat get in here? For that matter, how did *you* get in here?"

"The door wasn't locked; we just walked straight in," I said.

Rosie drew herself up, looking affronted. "I brought a client through the house yesterday, and I assure you, I locked the door."

This is your cue, I said to Syl. *Get out here and look half-starved.*

But she knows me!

I shrugged, ignoring Syl's objections. "Must be something faulty with the lock."

Rosie opened her mouth to argue when Syl bolted across the room and into the kitchen, startling a small scream out of her.

"There it is!" I said. "Open the back door, Lucas—it might run outside."

Lucas and Syl both took the hint, and in a moment, the poor, trapped cat had disappeared into the backyard.

Still frowning, but no longer quite as suspicious, Rosie turned to me. "That looked a lot like your cat."

"It did, didn't it?" I agreed. Thank God—or Zeus, or whoever—the crisis had been averted. "I guess most black cats look alike. The poor little thing—I wonder how long it's been trapped here?"

"Well, it certainly wasn't here yesterday," Rosie said, with renewed annoyance. "How on earth did the stupid thing get in here anyway?"

"Search me."

"It was very good of you and your friend to try to help it," Winston said, speaking for the first time. He sounded sincere, and I couldn't tell if it was an act or not. He'd seen Syl in cat form only the day before, and he knew perfectly well she was a cat shifter. "The poor thing could have starved to death in here."

Rosie took a deep breath and offered him her professional real estate agent smile. I had a feeling she'd forgotten he was there, and was now rather guiltily realising that this was no way to sell houses to people. "Yes, very kind."

He wandered into the kitchen and started opening cupboards. "What a delightful outlook from this window!"

With a last puzzled glance at me, she followed him. "Yes, the kitchen gets plenty of light, and as you can see, it's fully stocked with crockery, glassware and utensils. The last tenant left in a hurry, so the owner is happy to throw in everything left behind as part of the deal, to save him having to clear it out. The house is a great size for you, and the yard isn't too much work. Let me show you the master bedroom."

She marched off in the direction of the bedrooms. Winston winked at me, then followed obediently. Well, I guess that answered the question of whether he believed our little charade or not. I had to smile. Winston was just full of surprises.

Lucas rejoined me and we headed out the front door. Neither of us spoke until we were out on the street again. Rosie's little car was parked there. I couldn't believe we hadn't even noticed it driving up. What a fustercluck.

"There's never a dull moment around you, is there?" Lucas said.

I strode off down the footpath toward Syl, who was sitting on the front fence of a house further down the street, swinging her legs idly as she waited. "Glad you enjoyed yourself. Thanks for the back-up in there, by the way. So nice of you to run and leave me."

He grinned, not the least bit put off by my sarcasm. "You should have seen the look on your face."

Syl stood up as we drew level with her. "Most black cats look alike? Really?"

"What else was I going to say? You were no bloody help."

"Shame we didn't find anything," Lucas said, putting his arm around Syl's shoulders. "What are we going to do now?"

Syl smiled up at him with such a light in her face it caught my breath. Despite the height difference, they looked as though they belonged together. Lucas unconsciously shortened his stride to match hers, and she settled against his side as naturally as if she'd been doing it for years.

"Stuffed if I know," I said, unable to keep the grumpy note out of my voice. "I'm open to suggestions."

It had so easily become "we" for him. I should be grateful, but the truth was that seeing them together only made me miss Jake more. When would I see him again? At the rate we were going, probably never. My one lead had just fizzled out, and I was no closer to discovering Hades' whereabouts than before.

4

"You're going to wear a hole there if you don't stop pacing," Syl said, eyeing me over the rim of her coffee cup with a sort of weary patience. She was stretched out on the lounge, and Holly was in the armchair, feeding Mireille. It astonished me how often that baby needed feeding—and how long it took. Holly had come in nearly an hour ago, because she liked to have someone to talk to while the baby fed, and they were still going. For most of that hour she'd been regaling Syl with stories about Lucas, and Syl was lapping it up.

I stopped moving and stared out the big window, towards the ocean. From here, a white sliver of beach was visible to the right. The wharves where the tourist boats were tied up lay in the other direction, and I could see a couple of the boats out on the blue water, probably on a dolphin-watching cruise. Usually, this view soothed me. I could sit on the couch where Syl lay, staring out at it for hours at a time. But today, it had lost its power. I sighed and checked my watch again. Still too early to try sneaking down into the cellar of the pub—I'd have to wait until the lunchtime crowd thinned out a little.

The front door opened and a man strode in. I'd been expecting Joe or Lucas, but it was Apollo. He wore all black, his shirt open at the collar, showing a tanned chest. It occurred to me that I'd never seen him wear any other colour—probably someone had told him once that black looked good against his tan. It certainly set off his blue eyes and blonde hair.

"Told you he wouldn't knock," Syl said, shooting me a triumphant glance as she got up to give him a hug.

Winston followed him in, looking a little awkward. He probably would have preferred to knock; he struck me as the kind of person who liked to observe the niceties. No doubt that was his years in the temple showing through—his life there would be governed by rituals and routines. He turned and shut the door quietly behind him.

Apollo returned Syl's embrace warmly, kissing her on each cheek as if he hadn't seen her for years. His affection didn't bother me now that Lucas was in the picture. I couldn't see her falling for the sun god's charms while the burly werewolf was warming her bed.

"I didn't expect to see you again so soon," I said. "Aren't you still busy rooting out corruption in the Ruby Palace?"

"You were right. I should have left more of them alive." He gave me a fierce grin. No kisses, though, which was fine by me. Despite the continuing danger from the shadow shapers, he looked happier than I'd ever seen him. Killing people must really agree with him. "The Ruby Adept and his immediate cronies managed to slip away. The ones that are left are either innocent or stupid, as far as I can tell. I'm having trouble finding out anything useful."

He said hello to Holly and admired the baby, tickling her tiny feet, before he dropped onto the lounge Syl had been sitting on. She sat down beside him, perfectly at ease with him. Holly, on the other hand, looked a little startled to find herself in a god's company, but luckily, Mireille was taking up most of her attention. Winston hovered awkwardly by the door. I wondered if Apollo had commented on his lack of priestly attire.

"Have a seat, Winston." I gestured at the other armchair, but he shook his head. Maybe there was some priestly prohibition about sitting in the presence of your god.

"Can you afford to leave the fireshapers unsupervised for so long?" Syl asked. It was a six-hour round trip from Crosston.

"Oh, I only ducked down for a moment." Seeing her confused expression, he added: "Winston's set up the temple. I can be here faster than walking from one room to another."

"Already? I thought he was buying a house?" Even if he'd offered on a house today, there would be weeks to wait before settlement. "Did you decide to rent instead?"

"Your friend Rosie arranged for me to rent from the seller until settlement," Winston said. "I have moved in."

"That's good," I said to Apollo. "At least now we have a way to contact you more easily. You should get a phone."

"And make it easier for my enemies to track me? No, thanks."

"Do you know where the Ruby Adept is?" Syl asked.

"There are rumours that he's gone to Brenvale." The god shrugged. "I suppose it's possible, but I would have expected him to flee to the human territories, if he's in bed with the shadow shapers. Not a watershaper city. If he thinks they can hide him from me, he's sadly mistaken. What's been happening here? Have you found out anything?"

"No. We thought we had a lead—a human we suspect of working for the shadow shapers left town suddenly just before Hades disappeared. We tried searching her old house, but we couldn't find any information there."

"Why do you suspect her of working for the shadow shapers? Just because of the timing of her departure?"

I described my chat with Rosie, and how Hades had seemed to find Becky's departure significant. I added that I'd sometimes seen her looking at shifters in an odd way, and had wondered if she belonged to One World—the human organisation that hated shifters and shapers—long before I knew anything about shadow shapers. Holly looked down at Mireille's sweet face when I brought that up, not saying anything. She had considered the woman a friend.

Apollo looked thoughtful when I'd finished. "You say Hades left town straight after he spoke to Rosie in the bar?"

"Well, I don't know if he left town or not, but no one saw him again after that, and I don't think he came back to the underworld."

"And when you and Jake were travelling back from your visit to Hephaistos in the underworld, Cerberus felt that his master was in danger and left you?"

"That's right."

"But that was some time later, right?"

"Yes." Hades had spoken to Rosie on the Tuesday night. I'd waited all day for him to return on the Wednesday. When he didn't, I'd taken the Helm of Darkness on Wednesday night—or, more accurately, the early hours of Thursday morning—and Jake and I had left in search of Hephaistos. We'd spent Thursday night at his house. It wasn't until we were on our way back to Hades' palace on Friday that Cerberus had suddenly panicked and run off and left us. "I guess it was more than forty-eight hours later. What could he have been doing for those two days?"

"No idea," Apollo said. "I find it hard to believe it could have had anything to do with this Becky person. What would be the point of searching for her *after* she'd told the shadow shapers all about him—if she was, indeed, working for the shadow shapers? Nothing he could do at that point would make him any less exposed. Chasing after her would only lead him closer to danger. And he's always been the cautious type, preferring to keep a low profile than get directly involved. If he knew his cover was blown, why didn't he just go back to the underworld where his enemies couldn't reach him?"

"And how *did* they reach him?" Syl asked. "That's the part I don't understand. We don't know how they're managing to capture gods, but Hades has an advantage over the other gods. If he found himself trapped, or felt threatened, he could have just opened a passage to the underworld and escaped. He can do that anywhere, any time, right?"

"Right." Apollo's handsome face was sombre. Perhaps he was reflecting on his own time in captivity. He might even be afraid for himself, that he might get taken again. Since we didn't know how the shadow shapers were capturing the gods, it was impossible to guard against them. "But I'm not convinced this Becky has anything to do with it. Her leaving is surely just a coincidence. He must have been about some other business."

"Coincidence or not, I reckon the end result is the same. Unless he suddenly decided to go on holidays and forgot to tell us, there's really only two options," I said. Gods could be fickle, and a bit careless of the passage of time, but Hades had to know we would be worried about him. He wouldn't have stayed away this long without at least sending a message if he had any choice in the matter. "Either the shadow shapers are holding him, or he's already dead."

A sudden silence descended on the room, as if everyone was holding their breath at once. Even little Mireille, fussing on her mother's shoulder, fell silent. Her dark eyes were enormous in her tiny face.

No one spoke, though they all must have considered the possibility. I can't have been the only one worried about it. "We should at least check that he's still alive before we go tearing the world apart looking for him. Where would we even start?" It could all be for nothing. I didn't want to face the possibility, but it had to be said.

Holly spoke for the first time since Apollo had arrived. "I think Becky was from Brenvale originally."

Apollo looked sharply at her. "Did she tell you that?" Implicit in his tone was the fact that you couldn't trust anything a mole told you. Why would she give any of her real background away? "It's a shaper city, so it's probably a lie."

"Not necessarily," Syl said. "There are plenty of humans

around here, and this is shaper territory. Maybe that's where she learned her hatred of shapers."

It wasn't hard to imagine. Shapers—and even shifters, to a lesser extent—had no trouble flaunting their supposed superiority over humans. She could easily have had a bad experience that turned her against the ruling classes.

"She didn't say so specifically." Mireille began to fuss, so Holly stood up and started the jiggling-and-patting routine that always seemed to follow a feed. She paced back and forth in front of the window, just as I had done, though she wasn't admiring the view. "I just figured it out from a couple of things she said about her childhood. And yes, I suppose they could have been a lie—part of her cover story, if she really was a spy—but we haven't got much else to go on. And it seems unlikely that she would have lied about everything. Keeping track of so much, all the time, would have been exhausting."

"If it's true that the Ruby Adept is holed up there, it does seem more likely," Syl said. "But she could just as easily have gone to Newport. We know for a fact that the shadow shapers have a base there."

Apollo tapped his fingers on the arm of the lounge, thinking. "The shadow shapers could have bases in a dozen different human cities. I'd be more prepared to believe that than that they have a base in the biggest watershaper city in the southern hemisphere. Forget this Becky. I'd like to know where the shadow shapers kept me imprisoned all that time. It was secure enough to hold me for a year—it seems likely that that's where they're keeping Hades."

"You don't know where you were?" Syl asked.

"No. I woke up in a cell there, and I never saw the outside of the building until they brought me to Newport for sacrifice. It didn't seem far from Newport by car, though, so I doubt it was Brenvale."

"Even if this Becky person has no connection to the case, my lord," Winston offered, "finding the Ruby Adept would most likely lead to the people responsible for Lord Hades' disappearance. Brenvale might be a good place to start if he is there."

"True." Apollo smiled approvingly at his priest, and Winston beamed with pleasure.

"Well, before we go anywhere, I'm going to speak to Charon," I said. "I'm just waiting until the crowd in the pub thins out, and then I'll head down to the underworld."

Apollo snorted. "The ferryman may not speak to *you*, after you assaulted him and stole his ferry."

I'd needed the famous ferry of the dead to save Jake, and Charon the ferry master hadn't been open to persuasion, so I'd "persuaded" him with a lump of metal instead. "He seemed okay about it afterwards."

"The ferry may not be in, anyway," he said. I glared at him. Why did he always have to argue? "I'll come with you, and we'll speak to Thanatos instead. He will know whether Hades is numbered among the dead."

"Who's Thanatos?"

"He is Death."

"I thought that was Hades?"

"No. Hades is Lord of the Underworld, king of the dead. It is a subtle but important distinction. Thanatos is Death itself personified."

"So he's, like, the Grim Reaper? The guy with the scythe?"

Apollo rolled his eyes. "You watch too much TV."

"Can he question the dead, too, like Hades can?" Syl asked. "Maybe one of the dead shadow shapers knows where you were held."

Apollo shook his head. "I think only Hades holds that power, but perhaps he can still help us. The Pool of Mnemosyne holds many memories."

The Pool of Mnemosyne—I'd heard of that before. My heart began to beat a little faster. Was it possible the Pool could return my own lost memories?

Mireille gave a belch so loud I could have sworn it came from a grown man, followed by a very wet noise. Something spattered on the floor and I turned to find Holly dripping with baby spew. Mireille had thrown up all over her shoulder and down her back. The burp cloth Holly wore on her shoulder hadn't stood a chance. It was hard to believe that tiny stomach could have held so much fluid.

Holly held the baby out away from the disaster area. Miraculously, none of it had ended up on Mireille herself. "Sorry about your floor. God, I'm a mess. I'll have to go change."

"Give her to me," Apollo said, coming to his feet in a smooth movement. Holly looked surprised but handed the baby over without comment and made her escape. He grinned down at the bright-eyed little bundle in his arms. "Do you feel better now, gorgeous?"

I exchanged a look of amazement with Syl as I went to grab some kitchen paper to wipe the floor. He held the baby expertly in the crook of one arm, patting her in a gentle rhythm with his other hand as he crooned nonsense to her. Mireille gazed up at him serenely, accepting his adoration as her due.

He caught the look I was giving him. "What? I've had children before. I know what I'm doing."

"So I see." I moved closer, drawn by the baby's dark eyes. So serious.

"Children are like flowers," he said, "come to brighten our lives with their joy."

Like flowers? What, they bloomed for a few days, then went brown and dropped bits of crap everywhere? I opened my mouth to harass him over his choice of imagery when I noticed the melancholy lurking in his eyes. Suddenly, I didn't want to know what had become of his children.

Unless they were gods themselves, they were probably long dead.

Maybe there were some sucky aspects of being a god.

I knelt at his feet to clean the floor. He looked down, then brushed something from my shoulder. "You've got some—oh, never mind. It's a tattoo."

I was wearing a sleeveless top that showed the tattoo on my shoulder. We hadn't spent a lot of time together, so he probably hadn't noticed it before.

He pushed my top out of the way so he could see it properly. "Why the archer?"

"The bow is my favourite weapon."

"Do you shoot much?"

"She shoots her mouth off all the time," Syl said.

"No, not recently." I gave Syl a dirty look. "Haven't had much chance."

"You'd get on well with my sister. She loves peppering things with arrows."

"I bet she'll be glad to hear you're free," Syl said.

A shadow crossed his face. "I've been trying to contact her since I got my powers back, but she seems to have disappeared."

That sounded ominous in the current climate. I hoped she hadn't fallen victim to the shadow shapers, too. From the look that Syl gave me, she was thinking the same thing. "She's probably gone into hiding," she said.

"Probably." His tone lacked conviction. He traced a finger over the curved line of the tattooed bow on my shoulder. I restrained a shiver—it felt like fire crawling on my skin. "I'll take you hunting one day, when this is all over." He bared his gleaming white teeth in another of those fierce grins. It looked odd with the baby in his arms. "One day when we've finished hunting down the shadow shapers, that is."

5

An hour later, I was back in the underworld. Lucas had started some kind of drinking game with a group gathered under the big TV in the pub. It involved a fair bit of yelling, some raucous laughter, and much slamming of glasses down on the table. I had no idea what they were doing, but the commotion kept all eyes firmly on the game, and no one noticed as Apollo and I slipped through the door marked "Private" and down the steps to the vampire's cellar.

Every time I came through here, I had to smile at the theatricality of Alberto's set-up: the great swathes of red velvet draped on the walls, the coffin on its dark plinth in the centre of the otherwise empty room. I moved aside the curtain that hid the elevator and Apollo and I stepped in. He ignored the obvious buttons on the panel by the door, instead going straight to the secret panel that hid the real buttons. He pressed the down button and we began our smooth descent into Hell.

The doors slid open on a quiet, carpet-lined hall. Apollo led the way through the silent house, past the paintings of the gods in the massive foyer, out the huge double doors and down the wide steps to the gravel drive. No one saw us, unless there truly were invisible servants lurking around, as I'd always suspected.

Outside, the fake sun of this part of the underworld shone down. It was warm enough for me to be comfortable in my singlet top and jeans, not much different from the sunny spring day we'd left behind. For a few moments, the only sound that broke the silence was the crunch of our footsteps on gravel, and then a deep, excited bark sounded from behind us. I turned to greet the owner of that bark as he galloped around the side of the building.

BOSSY GIRL BACK! he roared into my mind with his usual lack of volume control.

"Hey, Cerberus." Two heads butted against me so hard they nearly knocked me to the ground, and the third administered an exuberant licking to the side of my face. "Did you miss me?"

I really needn't have asked—it wasn't like he was greeting Apollo in the same way. In fact, he ignored the sun god completely. Apollo watched, grinning, as I tried to shove the enormous heads away without getting drenched in dog slobber.

LONELY HERE, he said, giving me an affectionate

nudge before finally allowing me to push him away. He didn't go far, though. He trotted at my heels as I followed Apollo along a familiar path toward the Plains of Asphodel.

Inevitably, my thoughts turned to Jake. Across that plain, one arrived at the laughing clown gate, and through the gate it was only a hop, skip, and jump to the ferry wharf where we'd first met Styx. The dark waters of her river lapped against the wharf there. If I stood on that wharf, would I catch a glimpse of Jake's dark head beneath the waves?

Before we even arrived at the plains, Apollo turned off down a side path I hadn't noticed before, that led in the opposite direction. I hesitated at the turn-off, glancing back in the direction of the wharf.

"Do you really want to give her the satisfaction?" Apollo asked. He had stopped on the path to wait for me.

I didn't need to ask who he meant. Was I that easy to read? "I just thought maybe I could see him …"

I trailed off. The expression on his face was sympathetic, but he shook his head. "You know she'd never let you, but the fact that you tried would absolutely make her day. Don't waste your time, Lexi. You've got more pride than that."

I nodded and joined him on the new path. He was right. I'd rather eat a dead rat than do anything that made that bitch Styx happy. Soon, we would free Jake. But first, we had work to do.

We left the artificial daylight of the area around Hades' palace, and the ever-present mist began to rise, drifting around our feet as we walked. It was dark here, but not pitch-black—only dark enough to add to the underworld's creepy vibe. Apollo started glowing as we walked, until he was casting quite a serious light.

"Remind me not to take you next time I want to sneak up on someone," I said.

He snorted. "I can tone it down if you'd rather break your ankle falling into a hole you didn't see."

"Speaking of sneaking around—maybe we should go see Hephaistos and retrieve the Helm while we're here." Hades' Helm of Darkness, currently in the rather unimpressive form of a baseball cap, was nevertheless an amazing piece of equipment. Whoever wore it was completely invisible. A thief could hardly ask for a more powerful tool in her arsenal. I had rather reluctantly given it to the cyclops Brontes to allow him to escape the harpies who guarded Tartarus, with instructions to give it to Hephaistos for safekeeping once he joined his former master. "It could come in very handy if we have to infiltrate another shadow shaper stronghold to rescue Hades."

"I think it might be safer to leave it here."

"Why? Is it his avatar?"

Apollo hesitated before answering. "I'm not actually sure. Not all gods' avatars are as well known as Zeus's three-pronged lightning bolt, or Poseidon's trident. Some of us preferred to keep such information a little closer to our chests, even before the danger posed by the shadow shapers became apparent."

"But you think the Helm is Hades'?" It made sense. It was an artefact of great power, and had long been associated with the Lord of the Underworld.

"Indeed. I've long suspected that Athena's is her owl, and that Hades' is the Helm, but I don't know anyone else's."

"Not even your sister's?"

He smiled. "We may be twins, but we aren't very alike. Artemis's domain is the night, and she loves to keep others in the dark. My sister is rather suspicious of people."

"Whereas you're just the sunny, happy guy that everyone loves?"

"Exactly," he said, ignoring my sarcasm and giving me a sweet smile. "But anyway, to return to the point, we can't risk taking the Helm to the overworld. If you get caught with it, then the shadow shapers have Hades and his avatar, and that will be the end of him."

That touched on my professional pride. "I won't get caught," I assured him. "I'd be invisible."

He gave me an impatient look. Clearly, he didn't share my confidence. "Nevertheless, I think we must leave it where it is."

A black building loomed out of the twilight world, long and low, a row of graceful pillars along its front giving it the look of an ancient temple. If it had been sunlit, it would probably have been beautiful, but in the dark it projected a sense of foreboding, and the empty spaces between the pillars gaped like mouths. A heavy gate, also black, stood open, and Apollo passed beneath its arch without a break in his stride. I followed, a little more cautiously, my senses on high alert.

We emerged into a large, open courtyard where three ebony thrones sat on a high dais in the centre. No one was around.

"What is this place?" I asked.

"The Courts of Judgement," Apollo replied. "The dead come here when the ferry delivers them to the underworld. The judges decide what their fate in the afterlife will be. Most will drift in the Plains of Asphodel, their lives and sins forgotten. Those who have earned a hero's reward will feast in Elysium, while the very worst will be imprisoned in Tartarus, there to be eternally tortured."

I shuddered, remembering those red-lit caverns. Not a pleasant place to spend five minutes, let alone eternity.

Apollo let his brightness flare, chasing the shadows from the courtyard, and raised his voice. "Apollo, the sun god, is here to see Thanatos, Lord of Death. Let Thanatos come forth!"

A shadow broke away from the darkness beneath the archways and resolved into the figure of a man. He faded as he approached Apollo's brightness, and I realised with a shiver that I could see the outline of the building through him. One of the dead, then. "This way, my lord. I will take you to Lord Thanatos."

The dead servant led us down dark hallways, our footsteps echoing hollowly in the empty stone passages, until we arrived at a set of double doors. Light spilled into the corridor as he held open the right-hand door for us. I took care not to brush against him as I passed.

Inside, the room could not have been more different from the dark and dismal corridors we'd traversed. Coloured lamps burned in every corner of the room, and bright tapestries adorned the walls. A plump young man with a shaven head was seated at a large table, eating from a wide selection of dishes. Enough food was laid out to feed half a dozen diners, but there was only one place set.

He rose as we entered, wiping the back of his mouth on his silken sleeve. "Apollo! What a pleasant surprise. I haven't see you in an age—will you join me for dinner? Sit down, sit down. For a while there, I thought I was going to meet you in a professional capacity—I'm glad to see you managed to weather all that unpleasantness."

Apollo took the proffered chair, though he looked uncomfortable at the reminder of his brush with death. "It's good to see you, Thanatos," he said, rather stiffly. "You haven't changed a bit."

"I wish I could say the same for you, but you're looking a little peaky."

"A year's imprisonment can do that."

"Of course, of course. But what brings you here—and with such a lovely companion?"

His eyes fell on me as I moved toward the table. He was smiling, and seemed perfectly friendly, but a chill passed through me. I had no desire to come to Death's attention, yet here he was, waiting to shake my hand.

"This is Lexi," Apollo said, and I took Thanatos's hand, which was moist and fleshy.

"Pleased to meet you," I said.

Thanatos threw back his head and roared with laughter, making his double chin wobble. "Of course you aren't, my dear, but how perfectly delightful of you to say so. Don't worry," he added, when he saw my discomfort, "I'm quite used to it by now. I wear this form to try to make people easy in my presence, but still, the mortals can sense what I am. Death makes people uncomfortable, and there's nothing to be done about it. Now, you sit here, on my other side. There, isn't that cosy?"

I sank into the chair he indicated as the servant came back with two more place settings. Frankly, I didn't care how good the food looked or how much Thanatos pressed his hospitality on us. There was no way I was eating from Death's table—in the underworld, no less. That was just asking for trouble. I served myself a slice of pie, then sneaked it to Cerberus, who was stretched out on the floor at my feet, when Thanatos wasn't looking.

When the servant had finished and left again on noiseless feet, Apollo said: "We're here because of 'all that unpleasantness', as you put it. Hades has disappeared. Before we go searching, we want to know if he's dead. I figured you were the best person to ask."

"Goodness me! Dead? Of course he's not dead. He's the Lord of the Underworld."

"That doesn't make him bulletproof," Apollo said with some acerbity. "It's becoming more and more clear that none of us are as untouchable as we always believed we were."

"Things must be worse than I thought, topside."

"They are. But at least Hades is still alive. That's good news."

"That must mean that the shadow shapers don't have his avatar, then," I said. Because if they did, Hades would have been toast. That probably meant Apollo was right about the Helm, which was a shame. Its power would have been a great help—but it was a relief to know we still had a chance to save Hades.

"Surely it's possible that he's just wandered off on his

own affairs," Thanatos said, picking up a lamb chop in his fingers and biting into it with white teeth. Grease shone on his full lips. "Gods are always doing that. We answer to no one. What makes you think that he's in trouble?"

Apollo filled him in on what we knew of Hades' disappearance, including my suspicions of Becky and what we knew of her background, which wasn't much. He also talked about his own captivity and rescue, which took a lot longer. Thanatos became so interested that he stopped eating and leaned forward on his elbows, dabbing at his lips with a napkin as he hung on every word.

"You say some of these shadow shapers died during your rescue, in the collapse of the house afterwards? What were their names?"

Apollo glanced at me.

"One was called Irene," I said. "I don't know her last name."

Thanatos shook his head. "That's not enough to go on."

"There was also a man called Mike Newton."

The god of death nodded in satisfaction. "That, I can work with. Let's dip into his memories and see what we can find."

Apollo shot me a triumphant look, as if to say, *see? I told you he could help*. A thrill of excitement shot through me. The late, unlamented Newton had been Mrs Emery's right-hand man. Even though he'd died before Hades had been captured, the chances were good that he'd know enough about the plans and habits of the shadow shapers that his memories would be able to help us. Finally, something was going our way.

Thanatos wiped his mouth again and rose from the table. We followed him from the room and down a dim corridor, to a set of stairs. These wound down several flights before opening into another corridor, even darker than the last. Apollo didn't do his human light bulb thing, which surprised me. Perhaps that would have offended Thanatos; I wasn't up on the ins and outs of godly manners. I linked to Cerberus to boost my night vision instead.

I was soon glad of it, as the floor became more uneven and the walls lost their straight angles. We had moved into a natural passageway, which began to narrow. Apollo and I had been walking side by side; now we had to go single file. A soft, green light began to grow somewhere ahead of us. I was just beginning to wonder if Cerberus would be able to fit through when the passage widened again and opened out into a large, open space.

It was like a cross between a temple and a cave. Far overhead hung stalactites, like the teeth of some giant monster, but the floor was clear of stalagmites. Instead, most of the vast space was taken up by a pool, and the only sound was the occasional drop of water falling from the tip of a stalactite into the water below. A ring of columns that were clearly not natural formations circled the pool, holding up the roof. The whole scene was lit by a green glow that emanated from the pool itself, casting jagged shadows among the stalactites above.

I stared into the softly glowing water, watching as ripples spread from a tiny drop falling from overhead. The pool's surface moved in small rhythmic waves, far beyond what could be expected from the impact of one small drop, but I could see no fish beneath the surface, or anything else that might explain the disturbance.

"This is the Pool of Mnemosyne," Thanatos said. "The pool of lost memories."

Lost memories—I knew all about those. My heart began to pound. Was it possible the secrets of my own confused past were here in the unquiet water? I laid a hand on the reassuring bulk of Cerberus's shoulder to steady myself.

Thanatos took a ladle from a hook on a nearby column and offered it to Apollo. "Speak the name of the person whose memory you wish to recover, then dip the ladle in the pool."

Apollo went down on one knee by the edge of the water, the silver ladle clutched in his hand.

"That's it?" I asked. "He says the name and he gets *all* the person's memories?" I clenched my fingers in Cerberus's fur to hide their shaking. If I drank from this pool, would I finally understand my past? Would I know who I was, and where I had gained my strange powers? I sank to my knees beside Apollo, close enough to touch the strange glowing water.

"Well, it's possible to filter if you know what you're looking for," Thanatos said. "Hold the questions you want answered in your mind as you drink," he told Apollo.

The cold of the stone floor seeped through my jeans, chilling my knees, and I hugged my arms around my body as I watched Apollo. Gooseflesh rose on my bare skin. My heart pounded so loud I expected Apollo to comment any minute.

Instead, he leaned forward and dipped the ladle into the pool. "Mike Newton," he said.

Ripples raced across the pool, and the patter of droplets spilling from the ladle as he brought it to his lips was loud in the silence. I watched the droplets fall, and a shiver ran across the surface of the water. It was almost as if the pool were alive, as if all the memories it held animated it.

Thanatos was watching Apollo. Would he be angry with me? But I was here, and it was the pool of lost memories. Mine couldn't be any more lost if they tried. Damn the consequences. I had to try.

I dipped my cupped hand into the pool and brought it to my lips. "Lexi Jardine," I whispered, then I gulped the water down.

It was cold, sending tendrils of ice down my throat and

raising the hairs on my bare arms. I closed my eyes and held my breath, waiting. Waiting for the empty places in my heart and mind to be flooded with the warmth and light of knowledge, of memory returned.

I opened my eyes to find Thanatos and Apollo both staring at me.

"What are you doing?" Thanatos asked, a frown of confusion on his brow.

Nothing. Nothing had changed. A tidal wave of disappointment crashed over me, and I clenched my fists, furious with myself. What was wrong with me? "Why can't I remember?"

"What are you trying to remember?" Apollo asked gently.

I covered my face with my hands. They were still wet with the empty water. Empty of memories. Empty as my own stupid head. "Everything," I choked.

He handed the ladle back to Thanatos and put a hand on my shoulder. "You can't retrieve the memories of anyone who's still alive. The pool only contains the memories of the dead."

He stood, pulling me up with him. I stared down at the rock floor, fighting back tears.

"Did you find anything of use?" Thanatos asked Apollo.

"Yes. Brenvale is the shadow shapers' base, though they have cells in several cities. They started there and spread to

Newport, where Mike Newton became involved. Their leader is a woman named Mrs Emery, though Newton doesn't know much about her, beyond the fact that she is rich. She has a house in Sanctuary Point at Brenvale where I was held, apparently. I saw myself there." He shrugged, and I glanced up at him. His mouth was a hard line. It couldn't have been pleasant to relive his captivity through someone else's eyes.

Bad memories. That had been a terrible time for him. Was it crazy that I envied him his memories, awful as they were? At least he knew what had happened to him—there was only an empty hole where my past should be. I was still shaking, the pain of loss as fresh again as it had been when I'd first realised what a lie I was living. I clenched my fists so hard that my fingernails dug into my palms, trying to force my body to stillness.

"Newton rarely went there," he went on. "They liked to keep the different cells separate from each other, for security reasons. His boss, Mrs Emery, spent a lot of time there when she wasn't in Newport. If that was where they held me, it seems like a good place to start looking." He nodded at Thanatos. "Thank you for your help."

"My pleasure," Thanatos replied. "If there's anything else I can do, let me know."

They spoke more as we walked back up the stairs and through the long, dim corridors to the entryway. I walked behind with Cerberus, not paying much attention to their conversation, my head lost in my own miserable thoughts. We said goodbye to Thanatos and left the gloomy Courts of Judgement behind. It was almost a relief to step back out into the aimlessly swirling mist.

Apollo said nothing as he led the way.

BOSSY GIRL SAD? asked Cerberus, nudging me gently with one massive nose.

Yes, a little. I wasn't sure if he would understand my reasons, so I left it at that.

CERBERUS SAD, TOO. Red flames burned deep in his dark eyes as he regarded me solemnly. *MASTER STILL GONE.*

I know. I'm sad about that, too. I missed Hades. Even when his dry wit was turned against me, he was a comforting presence, almost fatherly. *But we got some useful information back there. Hopefully it won't be long until we find him.*

FIND MASTER? All six ears pricked up, and the very tip of his massive tail began to wag.

Soon, I promise.

Cerberus and I had slowed down while this conversation was going on, and now Apollo paused for us to catch up. He eyed me curiously as he waited. "Mind if I ask what all that was about back there?"

Should I tell him? I'd managed to keep my power secret from him so far, and I didn't know how he'd react to the tale of how I'd stolen his ring from Jake and run off with it to Newport in search of the source of my abilities. But what was I afraid of? That he'd strike me down for my temerity? Keeping my power secret was an old habit left over from when everyone I met was liable to turn on me for it. I had to keep reminding myself that I was among friends now, and power wasn't seen as a bad thing in the shaper territories.

My natural inclination to wall myself away and protect my secrets warred with the urge to speak. Apollo had proven himself, if not my favourite person in the world, at least a useful ally. Perhaps he knew something that would help me. I'd never know unless I spoke up.

"It's a bit of a long story," I said.

"I'm the patron of singers and storytellers," he said. "I like long stories."

And so, it all came out. I kind of glossed over the part about his own ring and how it had seemed to speak to me, but I was pretty open about the rest. I felt a weird kind of relief when I was done.

"I always thought there was something unusual about you," he said. "You don't feel quite like other humans."

"I'm an original." Jake had said something similar. I sighed. We were nearly back at the palace, and the way to the Styx. I knew I wouldn't be able to see Jake, but even so, my feet wanted to turn down that path.

Cerberus followed us inside the palace, his ears pricked anxiously. Apollo pressed the elevator button and the doors slid open, ready to take us back to the land of the living.

The hellhound whined as I threw my arms around his neck. "Goodbye," I said. "We'll bring Hades back to you soon."

FIND MASTER? CERBERUS COME, TOO! He surged forward, nearly knocking me over.

"You can't come, Cerberus. You're too big and obvious. We can't sneak around with a three-headed dog trailing us everywhere."

He stared at me, all six eyes flaming. A low rumble began deep in his belly, and for a moment, I thought he was growling at me. But then his body began to shake and I stepped back in alarm.

"What's the matter? Are you all right?" The rumbling increased, and his burning eyes closed. I glanced wildly at Apollo. "What's happening? What's wrong with him?"

Apollo shook his head, perplexed. Cerberus's skin rippled and heaved. His two outer heads leaned away from the central one, eyes still closed. With a great sucking sound like pulling a foot out of mud his body peeled apart. New legs appeared, and suddenly there were three much smaller dogs standing, blinking, in front of me.

I blinked back, shocked into silence. I'd seen some crazy things lately, but this just about took the cake. Each dog was still bigger than a Great Dane and had those red flames dancing in the depths of their eyes, but at least they had a better chance of passing for normal than a giant three-headed monster.

"Did you know he could do that?" I asked Apollo.

He shook his head. "That's a new one on me."

The three hounds regarded me pleadingly. *CERBERUS COME NOW?*

There were now three distinct voices in my head but the combination was just as loud as ever.

I stepped back and made room in the elevator. "I guess you can come after all."

6

"Oh, this is going to be good," Syl said when I walked into our apartment trailing three huge dogs behind me. She glanced at Apollo, who shut the door behind our little travelling circus. "I thought you guys were going to the underworld, not the pet shop. Tell me why the three biggest dogs in the known universe are cluttering up my lounge room?"

They certainly were crowding the space. One of them laid on the small section of carpet between the back of the lounge and the kitchen bench, effectively blocking entry to the hallway, though he curled up into the tightest ball he could. The other two stood in front of the window, trying to make themselves look smaller, heads hanging guiltily.

"That's Cerberus," I said.

"Really?" Her eyes widened. She took a deep breath and plonked herself down on the nearest couch, hands folded in her lap. "Okay, I'm listening. Tell me everything."

Lucas stood in the tiny kitchen, making coffee. "Wait. How did you get them … him … out of the pub without being noticed?"

"We didn't. Is there still water in that kettle? I'll have a coffee, too, if you're making them."

He cocked an eyebrow at Apollo. "You want one, too?"

"No, thanks. I'm not staying." He glanced at Winston, who was sitting on the couch, staring in fascination at the three enormous dogs invading the space. "We have things to do."

"Harry nearly had a fit when we came up out of the cellar," I said, accepting a hot mug from Lucas. My stomach was rumbling. We still hadn't restocked the fridge properly. I'd have to do something about that soon.

"She told him I'd brought my special tracking dogs to see if we could pick up the vampire's scent," Apollo said, giving me an exasperated look.

"Vampires don't have much of a scent," Lucas said.

"It was the best I could do on short notice," I protested. "Cerberus was a bit of a last-minute addition to the plan."

"Oh, we've got a plan, now, have we?" Syl asked drily. "That's good to know."

"We've got an address," I said, "which is even better, and we know that Hades isn't dead. It's in Brenvale."

"Road trip time!" Lucas said. He opened the door and called across the landing: "Joe! Get in here!"

"Brenvale is about ten hours' drive from Crosston," Syl said. "So more like thirteen from here."

"Is it? I've never been there." As far as I knew, anyway. There wasn't a lot of traffic between the big shaper cities. People tended to stick with what they knew, and watershapers were a very different kettle of fish to their fireshaping cousins. The only one I'd ever met was the mayor, and I'd often wondered what he'd done to get exiled so deep into fireshaper territory. "Have you? Is it true that all the streets are canals?"

"No, I haven't, but I used to work with a girl who was from there. And no, I think there are plenty of dry sections, but there are a lot of canals. So, tell us what happened in the underworld. Did you find Thanatos?"

Quickly, I filled the three of them in on our adventures. Joe came in while I was talking. He wasn't quite as tall as his younger brother, but seeing them together, there was no doubt that they *were* brothers. Same wavy hair, same brown eyes, same muscly build.

"So, what's the plan?" he asked.

"Road trip to Brenvale," Lucas said flippantly. The biggest difference between the brothers was in their temperament: Joe would never have broken into a house on a whim, which Lucas not only had done yesterday, but had thought it a great joke when we were caught by Rosie. "Can we borrow your truck?"

"My new truck!" Joe cast me a horrified glance.

"I promise we'll take better care of it than the last one," I said. "We need something big enough to fit Cerberus."

That started a new round of explanations, as Joe had missed the story of Cerberus's metamorphosis. Joe's new "truck" was a dual-cab ute, roomy enough for four people inside, with a big tray on the back. Hopefully the new slimline Cerberus would fit in the tray.

Joe eyed Cerberus, as if measuring him for size. "Do they all have to go?"

The three hounds turned their heads to look at him in the same motion, which was kind of creepy.

"I'm not sure how individual they really are," I said. "I wouldn't want to separate them."

"Perhaps my lord could transport you to Brenvale," Winston suggested, glancing at Apollo. "There is a small temple to the sun god there."

Apollo looked annoyed. "I'm not going near the place if the shadow shapers are there."

"Not even to drop us off?" I asked. "You'd only be there a moment. Surely you'd be safe inside your own temple?"

"You'd think so," he said, "but look at the fireshapers in Crosston. They're a bunch of backstabbers and fools—and that's the seat of the Ruby Council. If the shadow shapers could infiltrate even the capital so thoroughly, imagine what they could have done in their own stronghold."

"You still have plenty of loyal shapers," I pointed out. "Winston's not a backstabber, and he's a fireshaper."

"Winston's a priest. He doesn't have enough power to tempt them."

I winced a little at this dismissal of Winston's abilities, but it didn't seem to faze him. He listened politely, as if we were talking about someone else. "Well, the shapers in the temple in Brenvale are priests, too."

"This is not up for negotiation," Apollo snapped. "I'm sorry, but I won't put myself into danger, even for Hades. You'll have to take the long way."

I looked away from his angry face and met Syl's eyes. She shook her head ever so slightly. Okay, okay, I got the picture. He was scared. Even though I was cross with him, I could understand that. He'd been held captive by the shadow shapers for a whole year. It was probably the most horrifying thing that had ever happened to him in the whole of his pampered existence. Gods, by their very nature, were at the top of the food chain. They never expected to suffer, much less die. If the experience had left him with scars, maybe that made him a little more human. We all had them. It was called living.

Apollo stared out the window at the vista of the beach and the water stretching to the horizon. Darkness was falling, the blue leaching out of the sky and sea, fading to grey. Winston watched his god, his face giving nothing away. If he was hurt by Apollo's blunt summation of his lack of power, he gave no sign. It was a shame there weren't more fireshapers like him. He was loyal, and from what I'd seen, a fairly decent human being. He'd make a better Ruby Adept than probably half the former councillors. So would Jake, for that matter. I sighed.

Apollo cleared his throat. "I may be able to do something to help. When are you leaving?"

I looked at Syl and shrugged. "Tomorrow morning, I guess. No point driving all night and arriving exhausted."

He nodded once, sharply. "I've spent too much time away from Crosston already. I'll be in touch."

He left, closing the door softly behind him. We all stared at the door for a moment, listening to his footsteps fade as he went down the stairs to the street.

"That was odd," Lucas said. "Is he always like that?"

It occurred to me that Apollo might be embarrassed by his own fear—it was so very ungodlike—and I felt a certain sympathy for him. "He's a god. They're not like the rest of us."

"You can't expect him to be thrilled at the thought of going back to the place where he was held captive for a year," Syl chided gently. "Particularly when nobody knows how the shadow shapers are capturing the gods. He could be walking straight back into prison."

"I suppose so," I said.

"Don't be so hard on him. Why don't you like him?"

I shrugged, glancing at Winston, who pretended to be absorbed in the view out the window. "I never said I didn't like him. He's just … I don't know. Too pretty."

She laughed. "Jake's pretty, and it doesn't stop you liking *him*."

"That's different."

"Is it? Why? Because you don't want to bonk Apollo?"

"No!"

"Oh, you *do* want to bonk Apollo?"

Lucas and Joe burst out laughing, trading identical looks of enjoyment at my discomfort.

"Syl!" Was that a blush creeping up Winston's cheek? He was probably wishing he'd left when Apollo had. "It's different because Jake can't help the way he looks. And he's handsome, not *pretty*. He got lucky and won the genetic lottery. But gods choose to look the way they do—so why does Apollo go around looking like a member of a boy band? I reckon he's just up himself."

Joe folded his arms, still grinning. "You've got to admit, that's a compelling argument, Syl."

She smiled. "I don't have to admit any such thing. I think he and Lexi just got off on the wrong foot, and now she's struggling to justify her attitude, which she knows is unreasonable."

I rolled my eyes. "If you're quite finished with the

psychoanalysis, let's change the subject. Who's going to Brenvale?"

"Me," Lucas said immediately. He was leaning against the kitchen bench, a cup of coffee cradled in his big hands. He gave me a lazy smile.

"You do realise this is going to be dangerous?"

"You do realise I'm a werewolf?" He took a sip of coffee, his eyes laughing at me over the rim of his cup. "And also a bouncer. *Danger* is my middle name."

Joe threw his little brother an exasperated glance. "*Stupid* is your middle name. Sometimes I can't believe we have the same parents." His gaze softened as he turned to me, and a worried frown creased his brow. "I wish I could come. You need a responsible adult to keep an eye on you. But …"

"But you have other responsibilities, I know."

"It's just, with the new baby, and Holly not working, I need to put in extra hours—"

"Joe. It's fine. No one expects you to come." I grinned at Lucas. "We'll make do with the big, stupid werewolf here."

Lucas flexed his biceps and Syl fanned herself, pretending to swoon. I had to admit, they were impressive. The guy was ripped. Joe just rolled his eyes.

"So it's just the three of us, then?" Lucas asked, glancing at Syl and me. "Cool. We have beauty, brains, and brawn."

"Who's the beauty?" Syl asked suspiciously.

"You, of course, sweet kitten."

She frowned. "I should be the brains. We're doomed if we're relying on Lexi to be the brains."

"Have you looked in the mirror lately? How could you be anything but the beauty?"

I stuck my finger in my mouth and made gagging noises. "Don't forget Cerberus. He's coming, too." Then I appealed to Winston. "Are you sure I can't convince you to join us, and save me from these ridiculous children?"

Winston smiled. "I don't think I would be much use to you. I have no experience with these kind of intrigues. Besides, I too have other responsibilities."

So did I, for that matter. I sighed. "Me too. But I guess it won't matter if the bookshop stays closed for a little longer."

"May I make a suggestion?" Winston asked.

"Sure."

He looked at Joe. "Perhaps your lovely wife could mind the shop. She seems to be chafing a little at the restrictions of being at home with a baby. But the baby could sleep in a cradle in the bookshop as easily as in your home."

Joe looked thoughtful. "That's not a bad idea."

Ooh, I liked this plan. "Even if she only opened the shop in the mornings, it would be great, and it wouldn't disrupt Mireille too much," I said. Holly would enjoy chatting to the customers—it would stop her from feeling so isolated. "I've already been paid up to the end of the month—I can just transfer some money from my account to hers."

"Oh, we couldn't take your money," Joe said.

"Don't be ridiculous. She'd be doing me a favour. Of course I'm going to pay her for her work." And they needed the money, though I wouldn't say that. Joe had his pride. "Go ask her."

"I bet she jumps at it," Syl said, as the door closed behind him.

I did, too. I gave Winston a grateful smile. "That was a good idea. Thank you."

"I'm glad to be of assistance. If there's anything else I can do, please let me know—but now, I must be leaving, too."

When it was just the three of us again—well, six, if you counted Cerberus—I yawned. "We've got a long drive tomorrow. Let's grab some dinner and get to bed early."

Lucas grinned at Syl. "Sounds good to me."

"To *sleep*, Lucas," I said wearily. "Let's go to bed and *sleep*."

A pounding on the door woke me. It was still dark; I rolled over, disoriented by the sudden awakening, and checked the clock: 5:02. Too early.

Syl's door opened as I moved down the hall. "What's going on?" she asked, a shadow in the darkness. Something moved in the blackness behind her: Lucas, hastily pulling on his clothes.

"Don't know." My body buzzed with adrenaline. Early morning intrusions were rarely good news.

I opened the front door. Apollo stood there, fist raised to hammer on it again, Winston's face peering apologetically over his shoulder. Wordlessly, I held the door open, and Apollo strode into the apartment.

Winston followed him in. "I'm sorry for the noise. I told him it was polite to knock."

I couldn't help smiling at that, though my smile faded at the tense look on Apollo's face.

"You need to postpone your trip," he said. "I've just received a message from Zeus."

"What did he say?"

"'Hestia lightning'."

Syl yawned. "Hestia lightning? What does that mean?" She went into the kitchen and began filling the kettle.

Lucas appeared, shrugging into his shirt as he walked. "Is the road trip off?"

"Just postponed," I said, though I didn't see what difference this message made, if it even was from Zeus. "How do you know the message is from Zeus?"

"Probably because it makes no sense," Syl muttered.

Apollo gave her a sharp glance. She ignored him, too focused on taking coffee mugs from the dishwasher. Now that she was spending more time in her human form, Syl had rediscovered the joys of caffeine.

"The local school has one of those electronic noticeboards facing the street. It was congratulating the junior debating team or something—I don't know, I wasn't paying attention. As I approached, it switched to saying, 'Hestia lightning'. Who else could it be? As for what it means, I hope that she has some information about Zeus. If Hestia can help us get him back, we can strike at the shadow shapers and put an end to their schemes once and for all."

Lucas moved into the kitchen, his big body crowding Syl. Not that she seemed to mind. He nuzzled her neck, then grabbed two coffees and passed them to Apollo and me. "Who's Hestia?"

Some of the strain eased from Apollo's face as he took a sip. "One of the minor gods, now, though she was an Olympian once."

"She got demoted, huh?" said the big werewolf, snagging a coffee for himself. "That's pretty rough."

"She didn't get *demoted*." Apollo sounded just like his Uncle Hades when he used that testy tone. "She gave up her place voluntarily, because Zeus wanted to elevate Dionysius, but there were only twelve thrones. It was a noble thing to do."

"She might be in danger," Lucas said. "Maybe it means she's about to get hit by lightning."

Apollo made a scornful noise. "Zeus is not a fortune cookie. The lightning is his symbol. She has some connection to him."

"Could she be the one responsible for his disappearance?" Syl asked, pushing past Cerberus to get to a chair. One of him, anyway. I had trouble keeping his/their status straight in my head. Were they one being still, or three?

"You wouldn't ask that if you knew her," Apollo said. "Hera may be Zeus's queen, but Hestia is like a mother to us. It was she who helped Prometheus bring fire to mankind. She is one of the few gods I still trust. We must go to her at once and find out what she knows."

"Maybe I'll get dressed first." I indicated the skimpy pyjamas I was wearing.

"And have some breakfast," Lucas said hopefully. Werewolves were always hungry.

"Yes," Syl said. "Can't save the world on an empty stomach."

Apollo scowled. "I'm sure Zeus won't mind waiting until it's convenient for you."

"Oh, come on. Zeus has been missing for over a year. Another few minutes won't hurt. What's the rush? If you're in such a hurry, why didn't you just go straight away? Why come to us?" She returned his scowl with interest. "Maybe you're not as confident of Hestia as you make out. Maybe you want some back-up before you go visiting."

"From two shifters and a human? Don't insult me."

"Seems to me that you're the one doing the insulting," Lucas growled, moving to stand behind Syl's chair.

To Apollo's credit, he didn't react to the hulking werewolf's threatening stance. He ignored Lucas and spoke to Syl. "You don't have to come. I've managed all right the last few millennia without you. I simply thought to save you a wasted trip to Brenvale. If we have Zeus, then getting Hades back will be simple, and there is no need for any of you to endanger yourselves. But I can see I'm not welcome, so I'll relieve you of my presence."

He turned to the door, and I moved to block his way. "Get off your high horse, Apollo. Of course you're welcome."

I laid a hand on his arm. His muscles were taut with tension, and there was a hard look in his eyes I'd never seen there before. The poor bastard looked like he could do with a hug, though I wasn't volunteering.

I gentled my voice and smiled at him, giving his arm an encouraging pat. "Relax, would you? We're happy to come with you. Some of us are just grouchy because we're not getting enough sleep." I glared meaningfully at Syl and Lucas. It was ironic that *I* was now the one defending Apollo, after Syl's championing of him last night. "Oh, for

God's sake, Lucas, stand down. This is not a night club. Your professional services are not required."

Lucas rolled his shoulders, making a conscious effort to relax them. "Sorry." He looked a little shame-faced.

Syl went into the kitchen and started clattering around with pots and pans. I could tell from the way she wouldn't look at anyone that she was still cranky. Honestly, that pair needed to spend more of their time in bed actually sleeping.

Apollo's mouth was still a grim line. One of Cerberus shoved his nose into the god's palm. Apollo looked down at him and his face softened. He stroked the dog's silky ears.

SHINY MAN SAD? Cerberus asked me.

Yes, I think he is, I said, surprised at the hellhound's perceptiveness. Apollo had been angry—angry at being questioned, too used to having his word taken as law. But now, the anger had faded, and instead he looked hurt. For the first time, I wondered if he had any friends. He'd been imprisoned for the last year, and even before that, the gods had withdrawn from one another in fear and suspicion.

The smell of bacon frying filled the small apartment with its tantalising aroma. I took Apollo's hand and drew him gently to our tiny dining table. "Come and have some breakfast. We'll all feel a lot better with some food inside us."

There wasn't a lot of conversation over breakfast. Winston started a discussion about the town, which broke the ice somewhat, and asked questions about the best place to shop and the local attractions, which got Syl chatting. Lucas focused mainly on his meal, still looking a little shame-faced, though he very politely offered the salt to Apollo, who accepted it with equally excruciating politeness. I added something here and there, but mainly, I was thinking.

I'd love to rescue Zeus and have us all live happily ever after—I had someone in mind for my happily ever after, and I missed his smiling blue eyes. To have Hades back safe and well, to have everything go back to the way it was before, only better—it was the stuff dreams were made of. But it was a big dream to hang on two tiny little words. *Hestia lightning.* What did that mean? She knew something about lightning? Where it was going to strike? Like so many of Zeus's erratic communications, it didn't make sense. I remembered suddenly that odd text I'd received in the pub on Sunday, that just said "Hes". Maybe that had been Zeus, trying to tell me something about Hestia. The sender had been "Caller Unknown".

If only Zeus wasn't so incoherent. Still, I was all in favour of finding out what Hestia knew. Visiting her would only mean a short delay to our plans to find Hades, and it could give us valuable information. I wasn't quite so confident as Apollo that it would lead us to Zeus, but it was worth a shot. Besides, I was curious to meet another one of the gods. She was Hades' sister, wasn't she?

"Do you know where to find Hestia?" I asked as I cleared away the dirty dishes.

"I know where she was a year ago," Apollo said.

"But won't she have gone into hiding by now?" Syl asked.

"She was already hidden. Hestia was never strong. Hephaistos and I were the only ones who knew where she was."

"And if she's not there anymore?"

He shrugged. "Then it's back to Plan A."

Everyone got up, in a clattering of chairs. I went to get changed while Syl finished loading the dishwasher. I put on dark jeans and a T-shirt, and sturdy boots. Then I paused in front of the wardrobe. Should have asked where we were going. Would I need a jacket? I shrugged and put one on. It was easier to conceal weapons with a jacket.

I came back into the lounge room in time to see Apollo offer something small to Winston, with a casual, "This is for you." Winston gasped and took a step back, staring uncertainly at his god. Curious, I moved closer, to see what it was.

A gold signet ring lay in Apollo's palm. It had a design similar to Apollo's own ring etched into its surface—a sun with spiralling rays coming off it.

"My lord," Winston protested, "this is a high priest's ring."

"No, actually, it's more than that," Apollo said, still in that casual tone, as if it were no big deal. "I made it last night, to get Lexi to Brenvale, but she doesn't need it now. You may as well have it; it will allow you to travel between temples the way I do."

Clearly, it was a big deal to Winston. He put one hand on his chest, and I had a moment's worry for his ageing heart. "This is a great honour, my lord." His voice was very low; even though I was standing beside him, I could barely hear him.

"Simply a matter of convenience," Apollo said with a shrug, but I wasn't fooled. I was starting to read him better, and his priest's gratitude pleased him. "Use it to go to Crosston now and tell Adani that I may be delayed. He is to continue questioning the staff without me."

Winston's voice came out in a strangled whisper. "Tell Adani, my lord?" He cleared his throat and resumed in a more normal tone. "He won't listen to me! He's a councillor and I'm only a retired priest."

"Show him the ring; he'll listen. Take Cerberus with you, if you feel you need the moral support."

Cerberus's ears pricked up at mention of his name.

Can you guard Winston while we're gone? I asked.

For answer, all three dogs moved to flank the old priest. It didn't seem to help allay Winston's fears. He glanced at them and swallowed visibly.

"In fact, you can help Adani with his enquiries," Apollo said.

"Me?" Winston squeaked.

"Why not? You're a good judge of character. See what you can find out." He pushed the ring impatiently at Winston until the priest took it and slipped it on.

We left him there, the ring glittering on his finger, surrounded by black dogs almost as tall as he was, their red eyes gleaming. He laid a hand on the nearest dog's head, and three tails thumped the floor in unison.

7

I was glad I'd worn my jacket; the air was several degrees cooler when we stepped out of the tiny building that served as Apollo's temple in this area. Apparently, this was the fastest way to get to where Hestia lived. It was nothing like the temple in Crosston, hardly bigger than the lounge room of my apartment. Chickens roamed on the patchy grass outside the tiny temple, and a dirt road ran past the wire fence out front.

"Where are we?" I asked, while Lucas sniffed the air. It was heavy with the scents of pine and eucalypt, and had that moist quality that spoke of water nearby. The temple we'd just come out of crouched on the land in a huddle of rustic brick, no more than a simple, windowless cube with a sagging wooden door and a chimney centred on the shingle roof. Smoke from the sacred fire within drifted from the chimney into the pale blue sky.

It was just after dawn, and the birds were squawking up a racket in the trees that surrounded the brick box. There were no other buildings in sight and no people about, just the chickens scratching in the dirt.

"Somewhere in the Ridgeback Mountains," Apollo said, scanning the road for any signs of life. That explained the chill in the air. "Hestia lives about an hour away, over the mountain, but this is as close as I can get us. It's my only temple in this whole region."

"But it's shaper territory, right?" Syl asked. She was sticking close to Lucas, and I doubted it was just because she had the hots for that muscly werewolf body. The unease that I hadn't seen since Lucas had joined us was back in her face. We were a long way from home, and well out of her comfort zone.

"Of course," Apollo said. They didn't worship shaper gods in the human territories.

It hardly seemed as if they worshipped the gods in this territory, judging by the size and dilapidated state of Apollo's temple. I opened my mind to the life around us. The forest was teeming with it—birds in the trees, insects everywhere. Small creatures skittered through the leafy undergrowth, and possums and owls settled down to sleep in the branches above.

I ranged wider. A herd of deer grazed in a glade that sparkled with morning dew. A mother fox fed her cubs in a den beneath a towering gum. I found kangaroos and feral cats, wild dogs and wallabies. They showed me a forest that stretched for miles, and very little sign of human habitation.

"Hestia's place is this way," Apollo said. "Let's go."

It was a fine spring morning, with a nip in the air that made it perfect weather for walking. We followed him down the dirt road. Deep ruts in the road suggested that heavy vehicles used it regularly. Probably logging trucks. We saw no sign of them as we walked.

The exercise soon warmed me and I took off my jacket. Lucas kept casting longing glances at the forest on either side of the road, until finally he excused himself and disappeared into the bushes. "I'll catch up with you," he called, and a few minutes later, a wolf's howl drifted through the trees.

"I guess, living in Crosston, he doesn't often get a chance to run in a place like this," I said. Syl just shrugged.

"As long as he doesn't roam onto Hestia's land without us," Apollo said. "She may not take too kindly to having a strange werewolf rampaging across her property."

"I hardly think he's going to 'rampage' anywhere," I said. "He just wants to stretch his legs. Besides, you said Hestia was friendly."

"She is." But he frowned as he scanned the trees for signs of our missing werewolf.

"I'll keep an eye on him."

Syl gave me a startled glance; I hadn't told her that I'd let Apollo in on my secrets. But then, we hadn't had much time to chat lately. She'd been too engrossed with her werewolf chew toy.

He was currently barrelling through the undergrowth at top speed. Not hunting—he wasn't bothering to move stealthily. As I'd thought, he was just enjoying the chance to stretch his legs. I didn't link with him, just watched through the eyes of the forest as he soared over a fallen tree, his tongue lolling happily from his mouth. Birds flew up in alarm as he passed, but he paid them no mind, his long legs eating up the ground.

Twenty minutes later, he rejoined us, puffing like a steam train. The wolf emerged from the shadows beneath the trees, and two steps later, the man was walking towards us, a huge grin on his stubbled face.

"Better?" I asked.

"Much. I smelled smoke up ahead a ways. Would that be Hestia's place?"

"Probably," Apollo said. "I don't think there's anything else out here."

He quickened his step, eager to get there, but it was still a good half hour before we arrived at a track that branched off from the main road, barely wide enough to take a car.

"This is it," he said. "Another five minutes and we'll be there."

"I hope she's home," Syl grumbled. Her cheeks were flushed with the unaccustomed exercise. Usually, if she was travelling any distance on foot, she preferred to do it in her cat shape.

I shrugged back into my jacket, despite the growing warmth of the morning. Better to have my hands free and my weapons close. Just in case. I let my mind range out on either side as we followed the track up a gentle incline. I didn't like surprises.

I could smell the smoke that Lucas had mentioned now, though I couldn't see it. The trees pressed in closely on each side, leaning over the track and meeting in the middle so that we walked through a cool, green tunnel. A flight of white cockatoos screeched overhead, hidden by the foliage above us. I soared with them, enjoying the bird's eye view.

From up there, Hestia's house was apparent, nested in its own little ring of trees, with a large vegetable garden out the back. Smoke curled from two chimneys, one at either end of the building. It was a long, low house, and its black-tiled roof glinted in the morning sun like a snake's skin. A woman bent over the vegetable garden, a large straw hat shading her face. She was pulling out weeds from among the thriving plants.

I swooped away, borrowing the eyes of a lorikeet feeding on blossoms, then skipping to a small, grey bird that rested on a low branch beside the trail we followed. Uh-oh.

I drew closer to Apollo and spoke in a low voice. "There's a man hiding behind that big gum on the left."

"Alone?"

Reaching out to all the birds in the vicinity, I checked the cover on either side of the track all the way to the house. "There's another one closer to the house. He hasn't seen us yet."

They held no weapons, but they were probably guards. Shapers' weapons were their hands; they didn't need anything else. Both men wore the same uniform: a dark green shirt and pants in a heavy fabric, and sturdy black boots. Just doing their jobs. So far, they hadn't made a move towards us, only watched. There was no need to get twitchy.

And yet I was. I did *not* like being spied on; it made me feel vulnerable. The cockatoos had settled on an open patch of lawn in front of the house. I guided one to pick up the biggest pebble it could carry and brought it looping over the hidden guard's head. He nearly jumped out of his skin when the pebble hit his dark green cap. As the cockatoo flew back to rejoin its flock, I caught a glimpse of his puzzled face upturned to the sky.

Apollo stopped before we reached the big gum tree. "You there, behind the tree! Tell Hestia that Apollo is here to see her."

The guard didn't reply.

"He's fading back into the bushes," I said, watching as the man lifted a walkie-talkie to his mouth. "He's talking to someone, but I can't hear what he's saying."

"Good. Then let us proceed."

Lucas and Syl exchanged glances, then they both looked at me. I could tell they were uneasy, too. Walking head-on into possible danger wasn't my preferred option; sneaky was safer. But Apollo trusted Hestia, so we were stuck with trusting his judgement, though it made my skin crawl. I shrugged. "The coast is clear so far, guys. Let's go."

We fell into single file behind Apollo, Lucas bringing up the rear. His eyes flicked constantly from side to side and behind us, checking for threats. No one said a word, the air thick with tension. I watched from above, my viewpoint whirling through the trees like a dervish as I skipped from bird to bird, trying to see everything at once, until I felt dizzy.

"Our guy has joined up with his mate at the house," I said. Another man, dressed in the same uniform, came out to join them. They stood in a neat row, barring the way to the house, their arms hanging loosely at their sides. "There's three of them now."

"Weapons?" asked Lucas.

"Not that I can see."

At the head of the track, we stopped and faced the welcoming committee. The man in the centre stepped forward and flames sprang to life in his hands, which still hung by his sides. I almost laughed. It would take more than that to intimidate the *god* of the fireshapers.

"You're the man who claims to be Apollo?" he asked.

"No," said Apollo. "I *am* Apollo."

"Plenty of folk these days claiming to be gods that aren't," the man said conversationally. "Plenty of gods disappearing, too."

"Is he threatening you?" I muttered. "Are we still sure visiting Hestia is a good idea?"

"He's just doing his job, protecting Hestia," he whispered. Aloud, he said to the man, "Nevertheless, I am the real deal."

"And who are these others?"

"My companions," Apollo said unhelpfully. Maybe he could understand the man's barely veiled hostility, but he sure didn't like it.

The man raised an eyebrow. "Let's see some proof."

Apollo's lips compressed into a hard line, but he let his light shine forth. His body glowed so brightly I had to turn my head and blink away the after-image. "Proof enough for you?"

The man inclined his head in the barest of bows. "Thank you, my lord. You may enter."

We all stepped forward. Abruptly, the man raised his arms. "Lord Apollo only. Companions can wait here." He put a slight stress on the word "companions". Snarky bastard.

"Don't go in there alone," Lucas whispered urgently to Apollo.

"It's all right," Apollo said. "I'll be perfectly safe. It's only Hestia."

"Then why don't they want us to go in?" Lucas raised his voice and spoke to Hestia's guard. "Not acceptable. All of us, or none."

"Then it will be none," said the man.

Apollo folded his arms. "I assure you, little shaper, I could fry you where you stand. Only the fact that doing so would be disrespectful to Hestia is keeping you alive. Go and tell her Apollo wishes to see her *right now*, or I will decide to become disrespectful."

In response, the man's flames leapt higher, and flames appeared in the hands of his companion. Apollo's face went white with anger. Were they crazy, or did they have a death wish?

I stepped back, ready to duck behind Apollo when the char-grilling began, as a woman came around the side of the house. She wore jeans with dirt on the knees, an old shirt with the sleeves rolled up to the elbows, and a broad-brimmed straw hat. The men all released their flames and bowed as she approached. She took off her hat and fanned herself with it. This was the woman I'd seen weeding the vegetable garden—and also, apparently, Hestia.

"Apollo! How wonderful to see you!" She stepped

forward and stood on tiptoe to kiss his cheek, then wiped her forehead, leaving a smear of dirt behind. Her brown hair, streaked with grey, had been squashed flat by the hat. She looked to be in her forties, maybe early fifties. "I heard you had been captured."

"I was," he replied. "But now I'm free again."

"What a relief! Please forgive my boys. They get a little over-zealous in protecting me sometimes. As if I needed protection from you!" She laughed, and turned warm, brown eyes on us. "But who are your friends?"

"This is Lucas, Syl, and Lexi. Good to see you, too."

"Welcome." Her eyes lingered on me for a moment. "Well, you must all come inside and have a drink. It's already feeling warm—I think it's going to be another hot day."

Clearly *hot* was a relative term. There was still quite a chill in the air here in the mountains, compared to Berkley's Bay.

Apollo fell into step beside her as she led the way inside. She kicked off her work boots just inside the door. "Only because they're covered in mud," she said. "No need for the rest of you to take off your shoes."

The polished wooden floors were a warm honey hue, as were the exposed wooden beams. The colour lent a cosy glow to the white walls.

"Have you heard from Zeus?" Apollo asked.

She turned away to hang her hat on a peg beside the door. "No. Have you?"

"Yes. He told me to come to see you."

"Really?" She frowned. "What exactly did he say?"

"'Hestia lightning'."

There was a long pause, then she seemed to come to a decision. "Well, now. In that case, you'd better come this way. I have something to show you."

***

Hestia stomped back into her shoes and led us outside again. Her fireshaper guards had disappeared. We trailed after her as she went around the house and through the vegetable garden, past beds of dark green spinach and leafy carrot tops. At the back of the garden stood a small prefabricated shed. It looked ridiculously tiny compared to the much bigger barn behind it.

I wondered why they'd built a shed right next to the barn. Surely such a big building couldn't be full? But the shed was our destination. The door squeaked on its runners as Hestia slid it open.

I blinked, and held up a hand to shade my eyes. The inside of the shed was so brightly lit it was like staring into the sun—worse even than when Apollo did his light bulb impression. It took a moment of squinting before I could make out what was inside.

Hestia stood back as we all crowded around the doorway, staring at the impossible thing inside the shed.

"Zeus's balls," I breathed.

"Close," said Hestia. "Not his balls, but something almost as dear to him."

"It looks like a … is that—?" Syl faltered.

"A lightning bolt," said Apollo. "How in the name of heaven did a lightning bolt get into your back shed?"

The jagged white streak sizzled and popped, throwing sparks at the metal walls. It was embedded into the scorched earth floor of the shed.

"It didn't, actually," Hestia said. "We built the shed around it after it landed. Once I realised that I couldn't move it, I thought it prudent to hide it. I don't want anyone knowing it's here. But if Zeus told you, I figured it was safe to share my little secret with you."

"But the door wasn't locked," I pointed out, bemused.

"No one can steal it," she assured me. "You can't even get close enough to touch it. Try it, and see what happens."

No, thanks. Maybe I looked stupid, but that was an offer I had no trouble refusing. Apollo, on the other hand, stepped into the shed.

"Be careful," Syl said.

"I'm his son. Perhaps it will recognise me."

He stepped closer, and the shower of sparks increased. That didn't bother the god of fireshaping, of course. He took another step, and his hair stood straight up like a straw broom. "I can feel resistance," he said, "like trying to walk into a gale."

The lightning vibrated as he stretched his hand toward it, filling the shed with a sound like fingernails on a chalkboard. Abruptly, the two shifters moved away, identical expressions of pain on their faces, but Apollo forced himself another step closer.

That was it—the lightning bolt had had enough. Light burst from it as Apollo flew through the air, landing on his back in the middle of the carrots and spinach. Lucas offered him a hand up as Hestia slammed the door closed.

Apollo clambered to his feet, brushing dirt and leaves from his clothes. "I see what you mean."

"It's like that with everyone," Hestia said. "I nearly lost a man building the damn shed. Shall we go inside? Cup of tea, anyone?"

We trooped inside, through the back door this time, into a large, cheerful kitchen whose folding glass doors looked out over the vegetable patch, and beyond to the surrounding forest. A fire burned in a large grate—it looked as though it might have been used for cooking in the past, though the kitchen was equipped with modern appliances. We took seats at the kitchen table while Hestia put the kettle on. Apollo refused the offer of tea, staring out at the shed with a distracted frown on his face.

"Why is the bolt so small?" he asked.

Small? It hadn't seemed that small to me—it was the height of a man, even with part of it buried in the ground.

"You mean why is it only one branch?" Hestia asked, laying out biscuits on a pretty floral plate.

"Yes. Where is the rest of it?"

"That is the question, isn't it?" Hestia brought the tea tray to the table and poured for Syl and Lucas. "Zeus's lightning bolt is renowned as being three-pronged, yet here we appear to have only one prong." She shook her head. "One-third of the power of the father of the gods is sitting in my garden shed. I can hardly believe it. I've thought about it a lot, as you can imagine, and I believe I know what has happened."

She sat down next to Lucas, who offered her the plate of biscuits. She waved it away, all her attention on Apollo.

"We know how the shadow shapers work, how they steal our power by gaining possession of our avatars. I believe Zeus knew this, too. I think, somehow, they've attacked him and weakened him enough that he couldn't fight back. To save himself, he fled into the electrical system, and split his avatar into three."

Apollo shifted; an involuntary movement of protest. "I find it difficult to believe that Zeus's power wasn't enough to prevail against a bunch of second-rate shapers wielding stolen magic."

"I do, too," she said. "And yet they did it with you. If

they could bring the sun god down, why not the father of the gods? How were you captured?"

Apollo scowled. "I don't know. They did something to me so that I wouldn't remember."

"Then let's assume for the moment that my theory is correct. Zeus, in peril, and knowing that his power will be stolen if the shadow shapers manage to capture his avatar as well as himself, uses the last of his strength to split his avatar and send the three parts of it in different directions."

Lucas frowned. "And this happened a year ago, when Zeus disappeared? Why haven't the shadow shapers found the three parts in that time? They must be scouring the world for them."

"Because I don't think he just randomly flung them out into the universe. I believe he sent them to three people he trusted to take care of them."

"Maybe they *have* found the other two," I said. "This could be the only one left. Or maybe it was always the only one and they've had the other two all along."

"Maybe." Hestia gave me an impatient look. "But I prefer to think positively."

"Why did you never tell me you had this?" Apollo was doing his best not to look wounded, but I could tell he was hurt. After all his talk of how much he trusted Hestia, it must be galling to now realise that she hadn't trusted him to the same degree.

"I didn't dare tell anyone," she said. "Zeus's life is at stake, and I couldn't afford to get it wrong."

"Hmm." He stared out at the shed, frowning. "Who has the others, then?"

"I don't know. I think that's what Zeus wants you to find out. That's why he's given you this message, *Hestia lightning*. It must mean that he wants you to find the other two parts and bring them here to me."

That seemed like it would just create a magnet for shadow shapers. "What good would that do?"

"If we reunite them here, in a safe place, Zeus will be able to come back."

I pictured silver sparkles emerging from a power point, reforming in the air into the shape of an old, bearded guy. Or maybe pixels on a computer screen, merging into a likeness, which then stepped out of the screen into reality. The whole idea was bizarre. What had happened to Zeus's body, and what was he now? People kept talking about him hiding in the grid as if that made sense, but I couldn't wrap my head around it at all. Was he just currents running through the wires?

"If the other two parts are as unfriendly as the one you've got here," Syl said, "how are we ever going to move them?"

"We can worry about that when we find them," Apollo replied. "*If* we find them."

"So who would he send them to?" I asked. "Who does he trust?"

"Poseidon," Apollo said immediately. "My father is closer to the sea god than to any of the rest of us."

Lucas nodded. "Makes sense. They're brothers."

I barely managed to restrain a snort. Not all brothers were as close as Lucas was to Joe. Hades was Zeus's brother, too, but the dismissive way he talked about him made me think he didn't much care for him. He'd never mentioned being in possession of a lightning bolt. But maybe he wouldn't; Hades liked his secrets.

"Have you spoken to Poseidon about it?" Apollo asked.

"I can hardly go around asking everyone 'do you have a piece of Zeus's lightning bolt?', now, can I? People are going to get suspicious. Besides, Poseidon hasn't spoken to me in years. He's been holed up in that fortress of his since long before all this trouble with the shadow shapers started, refusing to let anyone in."

Syl glanced at me, and I knew what she was thinking. Breaking into fortresses was my specialty.

"But maybe if *you* turn up on his doorstep, he'll talk to you. He's always had a soft spot for you."

Apollo grimaced. "More for Artemis than me. He only tolerates me because she's my sister."

"Who do you think might have the other one?" Syl asked. "Who else is he close to?"

Hestia and Apollo looked at each other, as if each hoping that the other had the answer.

"No idea," Apollo said finally. "Most of the gods have gone to ground. We could search the underworld, I suppose."

Hestia eyebrows rose in surprise. "You know how to get to the underworld? Are you in touch with Hades?"

"Not lately," Apollo said. "He's disappeared."

"Oh, dear. Not another one."

"Poseidon might know," Lucas said. "Or he might even have them both."

"That would be wonderful." Hestia sighed. "I'm worried that Zeus doesn't have much longer. His messages seem to be getting more and more disjointed. If we don't get him back soon, he may be lost forever."

Well, that was a cheerful thought.

8

"Won't you stay longer?" Hestia asked, looking at Apollo with what could only be described as puppy-dog eyes. "You had nothing to eat or drink. You make me feel like a bad hostess."

We stood in front of her house, saying our farewells. The day was warmer now, though the sun had little bite to it at this altitude.

"At least let me save you a walk and get one of the boys to give you a ride back to the temple."

Apollo agreed that that would be a good idea, so the four of us soon piled into a four-wheel drive driven by a tight-lipped fireshaper. The bumpy dirt road wasn't conducive to conversation, which suited me just fine. Hestia had spoken of finding the other two lightning bolts as if it were something simple, but I could see us getting dragged into a quest that could take forever, and I was not happy. We didn't speak again until we alighted at the boxy little temple.

"Friendly guy," Lucas said, watching the dirt-covered vehicle drive away.

"The only good fireshaper is a dead fireshaper," Syl murmured under her breath, giving me a cheeky smile. I'd said those words plenty of times in the past.

"With maybe one or two exceptions," I said.

"You're getting soft in your old age."

We followed Apollo inside the ugly little brick building. Syl and I held his hands, one on each side, and Lucas took Syl's other hand. Together, we stepped forward and landed in the lounge room of Winston's new home in Berkley's Bay, our so-called local temple. There was no sign of the priest himself; only his acolyte hurried from a back room at the sound of our arrival. The poor kid dropped to his knees at the sight of his god, visibly shaking.

"My lord! How may I serve you?"

"Is Winston back yet?"

"No, my lord."

"I'd better join him, then." A look of irritation flashed over his face. "I need a decent Ruby Adept to manage things for me. I don't have time for this."

"If you'd had a decent Ruby Adept in the first place, none of this would have happened," I said. Or, at least, if the Ruby Council had been on guard against the corruption of the shadow shapers, instead of half their members lining up to join, the current situation would have been less dire. Maybe Apollo should have concerned himself a little more closely with what his followers were doing *before* it affected him directly. The gods had basically set the shapers, with their dangerous powers, free to run the world as they saw fit. It was no wonder things had gotten out of hand.

"You make it sound as though the fireshapers' disloyalty is my fault."

"If the shoe fits," I said. Syl gave me a horrified look, but I'd had enough of these so-called gods squabbling among themselves while the world burned. None of them trusted each other—even Hades, who seemed the best of them, knew a lot more than he was telling. Stupid Hestia had been sitting on that damned lightning bolt for a year, too scared to tell anyone else for fear of becoming a target herself, and now she'd dumped the whole problem in our laps. All I wanted was to save Hades and get Jake back, not get dragged into this whole mess.

Apollo took a deep breath, his nostrils flaring. "I'm going to pretend you didn't say that, because I'm going to need your … talents … to get me in to see Poseidon, if he proves uncooperative. First, I'll have to find out where he is, and then I need to finish dealing with the situation in Crosston."

"Didn't Hestia say he was hiding out in his fortress?" Syl said.

"It moves around," Apollo said, his voice flat. Not happy with me for delivering a few home truths. "Sometimes it's a cruise ship, sometimes a floating island."

"A floating island?" Lucas repeated, incredulous. "Wouldn't that be pretty obvious?"

"It's hidden by magic," Apollo said. "I'll have to make some enquiries. It should only take me a few days."

"A few days?" I said. There was no point in the rest of us sitting around twiddling our thumbs. "We'll go to Brenvale while we're waiting, then."

"No," said Apollo. "We'll need to move immediately once I have the information. Wait here for me."

"*No?*" The acolyte, still kneeling, blanched at my tone. But I was no follower of Apollo's. He didn't get to tell me what to do. "You'd leave your uncle in captivity so you're not inconvenienced?"

"It has nothing to do with my convenience," he ground out through gritted teeth. "Zeus is more important. Didn't you hear Hestia? We may never get him back if we don't act now."

"I'm saying we can do both. You do what you have to do; we'll go hunting for Hades. He's suffering. You know better than anyone how the shadow shapers treat their captives. Did you enjoy your year in captivity so much?"

"Of course not."

"So we can't just leave him there. What if you can't find

Poseidon? Why should Hades wait just on the off-chance that you might need me?"

"Fine," he spat. "Go, then, if you insist. But I won't be available if you get into trouble."

"Fine. When you see Winston in Crosston, tell him to send back Cerberus. He'll want to come with us to save his master."

A muscle jumped in Apollo's chiselled jaw. "Do you have any other errands for me?"

I folded my arms. "Nope."

The poor acolyte had his face buried in the carpet by this time, his body curled into a ball of obeisance. Apollo glanced down at him. "Remain here until your master returns, boy."

"Y-yes, my lord," the boy whispered, but Apollo was already gone.

Winston didn't show up until the next morning. At least it wasn't five o'clock when he knocked, plus he did it much more politely than Apollo had the day before. I couldn't imagine the serene Winston ever hammering on someone's door.

When I answered the door, he smiled tentatively at me. "I've brought Cerberus back. May I come in?"

"Of course." I opened the door wider and he stepped

inside, followed by Cerberus. All three tails wagged in the same rhythm. "Just because I'm pissed with your boss doesn't mean *you're* not welcome."

Indeed, I was very happy to see him—we were all impatient to be off. Our bags were waiting by the door, ready to be packed into Joe's truck. I was hoping it would be a quick trip, but I had a change of clothes, a couple of knives, and my lock picks. In the pocket of my jeans, the all-important key that Brontes had made nestled, ready to unlock the collar that the shadow shapers would have put around Hades' neck.

Syl and Lucas had gone for a walk on the beach, too impatient to sit still. I'd elected to wait, hoping Apollo wasn't too angry to send Winston back with Cerberus as requested. I knew the big dogs would never forgive me if I left them behind, and who knew what they'd get up to if I did? The thought of hellhounds running around unsupervised was more than a little alarming.

And now here they were. One of the dogs butted his big head against me affectionately, though he said nothing. I stroked his soft, black ears. *Good to see you again, buddy. Did you eat any fireshapers in the big city?*

SHINY MAN SAID NO, he replied, in offended tones. Seemed like Apollo was getting on bad terms with everyone lately. At least Hestia still thought the sun shone out of his butt.

"You're back in full regalia today," I said to Winston. He wore his official red robes, his hands buried in the long drooping sleeves. "What happened to those casual outfits you've been wearing?"

"I have a proposition for you."

"Really?" I arched a teasing eyebrow at him. "I didn't think priests were allowed to proposition young women. Aren't you supposed to be celibate?"

A tinge of pink coloured his cheeks. "A proposal, then."

I was more than half tempted to point out that he couldn't propose to women either, but decided to have mercy. That flush was adorable. "I'm listening."

"I know you and my lord had some differences of opinion about the best way to schedule everything that must be done—"

I interrupted. "If you're going to try to persuade me not to go to Brenvale, you can save your breath."

"Not at all," he said hurriedly. "I am completely in agreement that Lord Hades must not be left in the hands of those devils a minute longer than necessary. But my lord is genuinely worried. He would never say so, but I think he fears that you will not return."

What could I say to that? "The thought had crossed my mind," I admitted. "But I still have to go."

"I agree. But the quicker you go, the sooner you will be back, and ease my lord's mind." He held up his right hand, the long red sleeves of his robe falling back to expose the golden ring Apollo had given him. "I propose taking you there."

"That would certainly save a long road trip," I said.

"What would?" Syl asked, coming in with Lucas, their bare feet still covered in sand.

"Hitching a ride to Brenvale. Winston is offering to get us there via magic ring."

"Cool," Syl said, giving Winston a smile. "It'll make Joe a happy man if we don't have to borrow his truck."

"Are you sure you won't get into trouble?" I asked. "Apollo's not exactly happy with me at the moment."

Winston shrugged. "Perhaps today he will be angry because he is cranky with you. But tomorrow he will remember that you are his friends, and then he will be happy that I helped you." A small smile tugged at his mouth. "I will tell him tomorrow."

I laughed. "I like the way you think."

Ten minutes later, we stepped onto the stone floor of another temple. This one was certainly more impressive than the last, tiny one we'd visited. It was nowhere near as big as the great temple in Crosston, of course, but smooth columns held up a ceiling satisfyingly far above our heads, and the central fire pit was wide and deep.

The temple was long and narrow, rather than circular, and a large statue of Apollo loomed against the far wall. The god was sitting in judgement, with a scroll in one hand and a set of scales in the other, and looked regal and imposing, his golden curls lying in neat ringlets on his shoulders. A handful of people knelt before the statue in prayer. They had their backs to us, so they didn't see us appear out of thin air, four people all awkwardly holding onto each other and three large black dogs. The priest stirring the coals of the sacred fire, however, visibly started, and almost dropped his poker.

His thin face drew into a frown of suspicion, and he held the poker out in front of himself, not exactly brandishing it at us, but looking as though he was ready to use it against these strange intruders if required. "Who are you?"

His voice wavered a little on the last word. He was younger than Winston, but still middle-aged.

"I am the envoy of our Lord Apollo," Winston said, spreading his hands wide in a gesture of benediction. Or maybe it was to show that he was unarmed. Two of the supplicants kneeling before the statue sneaked furtive looks over their shoulders at his words. The other must have been truly desperate for the god's intervention, as he didn't move. I could have told him not to bother; Apollo was way too caught up in his own affairs to answer anyone's prayers.

The other priest's gaze flicked to Winston's right hand, where Apollo's ring glittered, and his stance relaxed slightly. The point of the poker sagged toward the floor. He jerked his head at the rest of us. "And who are they?"

"Friends of his," Winston replied succinctly.

The thin priest offered us a slight bow, and a deeper one to Winston, who did indeed look imposing in his red robes. I could see now why he'd worn them. Combined with the ring, they gave him an authority that the other man didn't question.

"Welcome to our temple," he said. "How may we serve you?"

The two supplicants had now given up any pretence of praying and were standing, whispering to each other as they watched us. Sound carried well in the large stone room; they could hear every word we said. I glanced at Winston, hoping he wouldn't give too many details to the priest. The man was probably a devoted servant of his god, but he had a sharp, pointed face that reminded me of a weasel's.

"Do you have guest lodgings here?" Winston asked.

"That won't be necessary," I said hastily. My plan was to disappear into the city, not set up in such a public location.

"Any friends of Lord Apollo are most welcome," Weasel Priest said. He could hardly keep his gaze on my face as he spoke; he kept glancing at Winston's ring. The poor man was probably bursting with questions—he'd seen us step out of thin air right in front of him. As far as I knew, Apollo had never created such a ring before, but the man would realise where its power had come from. He must be dying to know who Winston was, and why he'd qualified for such an honour. "What is your purpose here? Perhaps we can help you."

"They are on our lord's business," Winston said, "and it is none of yours." Ooh, snap. Atta boy, Winston.

Weasel Priest offered an apologetic bow, which Winston proceeded to ignore.

"Good luck," he said to me. "Let me know when you are ready to make the return trip."

"How will I contact you?" I asked, imagining some kind of archaic summoning ritual at the sacred fire.

He smiled. "Unlike my lord, I have a phone. Let me give you the number."

9

Through the doors of the temple, a strange sight awaited us. I'd thought the Great Temple of Apollo in Crosston had been fancy, but Poseidon's worshippers had left that in their dust. The temple they had built for their god was directly opposite us as we came out onto the steps, on the other side of a broad plaza, and it dwarfed the building behind us.

It was tall and slender, made of white stone that sparkled in the morning sun, and someone—or most likely, a whole army of someones—had carved an idiot's guide to the fish of the world into its gleaming surface. Whole schools of them cavorted across its surface, chased by whales and sharks and a few things I sincerely hoped existed only in the fevered imagination of the sculptors. I shaded my eyes, staring at the thing in awe. Here, I could make out a finned Merrow child peeking out from behind some coral; there, a pod of dolphins leaping playfully from the water.

In case there was any doubt about which god the building was dedicated to, a gigantic Poseidon reared from the waves at the top of the main tower, a golden trident clenched in his mighty fist. A lake surrounded the whole, with only a narrow causeway connecting the front doors of the temple to the plaza between us. Fountains in the lake sent water shooting high into the sky, there to form shapes of dolphins and other sea creatures before plunging back down.

"Well, I guess there's no doubt this is a watershaper city," I said. "Although I'm pleasantly surprised—I was expecting a lot more water. I thought there were supposed to be canals."

"Oh, there are plenty of canals," a voice said behind me. It was the Weasel Priest. "This is Temple Square. All the gods have temples here."

I dragged my attention from Poseidon's flamboyant temple and looked properly at the other buildings. Poseidon had one side of the square to himself, but the other three were taken up by nearly a dozen other temples, all much smaller than Poseidon's. There must be one for every Olympian.

"This is the biggest piece of dry land in the whole of the Old Quarter. Once you leave here it's nothing but canals until you reach the New City. Where are you headed?"

"Do we need a boat, then?" Lucas asked, ignoring the man's not-very-subtle attempt to discover our business.

"You can walk if you have to," he said. "There are paths along the edges of some canals, and alleys between buildings, but water is the most direct route. You should probably hire a boatman to take you where you want to go. It's very easy for strangers to get lost here."

Lucas caught my eye and shook his head slightly. I agreed. No boatmen. The fewer people we talked to the better. I thanked Weasel Face for the information and we set off across the square, steering a path between Athena's temple and a tiny building dedicated to Hera and Hestia. Figured—they'd shoved the two most often overlooked goddesses into the one temple.

"Do you have any idea how to find this place?" Syl asked, as the walls of Athena's temple loomed over us.

I was glad to get out of the square. Too many people had stared at the three huge black dogs trailing us, all three marching in step like a circus act. I looked back as we left it behind, and saw two of the suppliants leaving Apollo's temple. The other had stopped to chat with Weasel Face, and both were watching us.

"I guess we'll just find a car hire place and wing it from there." I nabbed a few pigeons and sent them soaring over the watery city, looking for what I needed. From the air, the city appeared to have been designed by a drunk, with canals zigzagging in all directions. Buildings sprung up between them with little rhyme or reason, crammed into any available dry space. I even saw one that was triangular, clinging to a tiny space where three canals converged.

The canals were full of traffic, though all of it was man-powered. Some people stood and propelled their flat-bottomed boats with long poles that they drove into the bottom of the canal. Others rowed. Nowhere did I see a single motorboat or hear the roar of an engine. The only engine noises I could hear were faint, coming from cars in the distant New City. Here in the Old, the lap and slap of water and the cries of the boatmen filled the air.

Every home or business that we passed had a small jetty out front with a boat tied up to it. Small lanes ran among the buildings, but they weren't wide enough for vehicle access, so people either walked or took to the canals. I thought about stealing a boat as we trudged along narrow lanes, but the canals were too busy, filled with the splash of oars and the voices of the boatmen as they navigated the waterways.

I had one of my pigeons circle round to check on Weasel Face. After the debacle in Crosston, every fireshaper was suspect. If he was in league with the shadow shapers, he could even now be telling them of the strange new arrivals in the city.

I saw the skirt of his white robe disappearing back into the gloom of the temple. Perhaps he was a loyal child of Apollo, going back about his business. Or perhaps he was heading inside to grab a phone and rat us out to the shadow shapers. It was impossible to tell using pigeon-cam. All I could say was that he hadn't followed us across the square, despite his apparent interest in where we were going.

I could *not* say that, however, for the supplicant who had stopped to speak with him on the steps. He was halfway down the alley we'd taken between the two temples, hot on our heels. Dammit.

"May the fleas of a thousand camels infest his armpits," I muttered.

"What's wrong?" Syl asked.

"We've got a tail. Why is nothing ever easy?"

She and Lucas both looked back, but the guy was too careful to be seen.

"I can make it easy," Lucas growled, the yellow of the wolf glowing in his eyes.

"He might not be working for the shadow shapers," Syl said. "Maybe the watershapers like to keep an eye on odd visitors to their city."

"Who are you calling odd, you weirdo?" But my mind was only half on the conversation; the other was in the air, watching our stalker, plotting our way through the chaotic alleys and paths of the watershaper city.

"Doesn't matter who he works for," Lucas said, "we still don't want him following us."

"Hold that thought for a little longer," I said. "There's

too many people here. We're coming up to a quieter patch."

A small, localised wave was moving down the canal beside us, pushing a large boat before it. A man and a woman sat in the back, deep in conversation. One of them must be a watershaper. No one was steering the boat—in fact, it had no wheel or rudder that I could see, and yet it navigated deftly through the traffic on the busy canal. I did notice that a lot of the smaller boats did their best to get out of the way. Perhaps watershapers weren't always as careful as they could be of other users of the waterways.

A smaller canal branched off the main one, and we followed it around a corner. The way was gloomier, the tall buildings on either side of the water seeming to lean over it and block out the sun. It was a long way to the nearest jetty. The canal walls, covered in moss and grime, rose high above the water. A lone boatman poled his boat through the green gloom, almost out of sight further down the canal.

I turned into an alleyway and stopped. "This would be a good spot for a swim."

Lucas nodded, and moved to stand at the very corner, a predatory gleam in his eye. I watched our stalker through the eyes of a bird on the roof of the building across the canal. After a long pause, he rounded the corner from the main canal. When he realised we were no longer in sight, his stride lengthened, and he hurried towards the alley where we waited. When he was close enough, I nodded to Lucas and the werewolf stepped abruptly around the corner.

A cry of surprise was followed by a splash as our friend took an unscheduled dip. Lucas looked pleased with himself when he rejoined us.

"Let's go," I said. "It's still a long way."

Weasel Face had told us that real roads began away from the temple precinct, but I hadn't realised quite how long it would take to get there through the chaotic Old Quarter. Cerberus drew many curious and fearful glances on the way, and I began to regret bringing him. We were too noticeable. Any of these people could be shadow shapers, or informants. Three such huge dogs were unusual enough to be reported. I was dizzy, trying to watch every direction at once, suspecting everyone I saw—but at least no one else followed us.

I tried to quiet my fears. Maybe they would think he was some kind of shifter. And even if the shadow shapers heard of him, why would they assume he was linked to the giant three-headed dog that had attacked them in Newport? They had no idea he could split himself into three. But every person who stopped to stare as we passed added to my unease. It was a relief to hear the sounds of normal traffic at last, and to find the car rental place.

"About time," Syl said. "My feet are killing me."

She and I waited outside with Cerberus while Lucas went in to hire a ute. There was an older model in the carpark with a bench seat that the three of us could squeeze into. The tray looked big enough to take all three of Cerberus, though Lucas didn't mention to the man behind the desk that he intended to load up the back with hellhound. In fact, there wasn't much conversation at all. He said hello as he walked in, and then I heard the guy ask what he was doing in town.

"Minding my own business," Lucas replied, in a dangerous tone that dared the other man to ask another question.

He didn't. Silence reigned until Lucas came out, whistling, with the keys in his hand.

Driving proved to be a frustrating exercise in the watershaper city, with the roads almost as haphazard as the canals had been. An hour later, Lucas slammed his hand on the steering wheel in frustration. "This place is a nightmare."

A map had come with the car, but I'd lost count of the number of times we'd got turned around. So many streets seemed to dead-end into canals. There weren't nearly enough bridges.

"I'm sick of the sight of bloody water," Syl said.

It wasn't restricted to the canals. Every second house boasted a fountain, or an elaborate ice sculpture. Despite the warmth of the sun, they didn't melt, held in place by watershaping magic. Many of the larger buildings had what could only be called icicles hanging from their roofs, though they were like no icicles I'd ever seen before. They swirled and split, forming intricate, lace-like patterns.

"It *is* a watershaper city," I pointed out. "You'd have to expect there to be a bit of water."

"What have the bastards got against bridges?" she said. "They can keep their stupid water, just give me a way to get over it."

I shrugged. "They're shapers. Other people's convenience isn't high on their list. The canals suit them, so why would they care?"

The sun was high overhead by the time we fought our way through the maze of the New City and out into the suburbs. Once we'd made it to the general vicinity of the shadow shapers' address at Sanctuary Point, we checked into the first motel we saw.

Much to his disgust, I hustled Cerberus inside, out of sight. "We're going to have a quick look at this place in daylight," I said. "Just to find out where it is. You stay here until we get back."

He sat down, all three of him in a row, staring at me with mutinous red eyes. I sighed, and put my arms around the nearest neck. Even sitting down, he was nearly as tall as I was. He just stood out too much. There was no point drawing attention to ourselves before we'd even begun. "Please, buddy. I promise we'll come back for you before the fun starts."

He grunted and licked my neck, which I took as agreement.

Back in the car, the three of us headed for Sanctuary Point. There was plenty of water here, too, but the roads were wider and easier to navigate. Sanctuary Point turned out to be an enclave of luxury homes on narrow fingers of land with a network of canals running between them. Each "finger" ran off the central spine of a broad avenue.

Most of the homes were on huge blocks, but there wasn't much to see from the street due to the walls that shut out the rest of the world from millionaires' paradise. Each property boasted a huge fence, often with cameras mounted on top. Some offered glimpses of the luxury within through wrought-iron gates, but most seemed to value their privacy too much to let the lesser mortals catch even a glimpse of their extensive grounds, all hidden behind solid steel or timber gates.

The house we were interested in was near the end of one such row. We drove past and turned around at the end of the street, then cruised past again. Two cameras sat above its gate, one on each side, watching the street with their electronic eyes. They would likely think us tourists out to gawk at the rich, if they took any notice of our lowly rental car at all.

I latched onto a flock of rosellas nearby and sent them whirling over the wall. The grounds were massive. That was no surprise. I took quick stock. Plenty of trees, though there was a clear zone around the house, unfortunately. A tennis court, but no pool? That seemed odd, until I caught a flash of blue on the second storey. Nice. The swimming pool was built into the side of the house. Hope they didn't have any leaks. That would be a bastard to fix. I wondered what was underneath it—garages, perhaps?

The house itself was huge. Three storeys of luxury, balconies and terraces all round, plenty of glass so the lucky occupants could admire the view. Was Hades looking out one of those windows right now?

Unlikely. They'd have him locked away somewhere, if he was here. They'd be even more nervous than usual after Apollo's prison break—the last thing they wanted was a repeat performance.

"See anything interesting?" Syl asked, as we drove away down the street.

"Big grounds," I said. "Fences on three sides, but it's open to the water." Strange that there was no security on that side, but I supposed they didn't want to spoil their million-dollar view. The house was situated to make the most of it and the access to the canal. The canals here were much wider than they'd been in the city centre, and they all fed into a sheltered bay. The smell of sea salt came in the open car windows, giving me a sudden pang of homesickness for Berkley's Bay. "There's a decent-sized boat shed next to the jetty, but no boat."

"They're probably using it."

"Probably. Let's come back tonight and approach from the water. I don't need to get close to their cameras to have a good look inside."

They agreed to come back after dark, so we returned to the motel. After lunch, I laid on the too-soft mattress in my room and tried to sleep. Cerberus approved of this idea and stretched out all over the room, crowding the floor with dog. Syl and Lucas retired to their room but, judging from what I could hear through the thin wall that separated us, they weren't trying to sleep.

I sighed and tried not to think about Jake. Soon. Just one more big effort and I would see him again.

10

We hit a takeaway joint for dinner once it got dark. Syl got a funny look from the guy behind the counter when she asked him why there were no motorboats on the city's canals.

"Shapers won't allow them," he said. "Too noisy."

Figured. Watershapers didn't need them, so why would they make life easier for the others who lived in their city? We saw one as we walked back to the motel beside a well-lit canal. Or, at least, we saw his boat. It was a large cruiser, with a group of people drinking champagne on the rear deck. A small wave rose up behind the boat, constantly renewed, pushing it down the canal at a great rate, leaving the other muscle-operated rowboats and punts rocking in its wake.

At midnight, we figured it was late enough to make our move. The city was considerably quieter as we took to the road. We turned off before we reached the house, and parked near an access point to the canal. Cerberus leapt down from the tray when we got out. The car rocked almost as much when his weight left it as those little boats had.

We were in the parking lot of a small park. A children's playground loomed out of the darkness, deserted now, of course. A few scattered trees probably provided nice shady picnicking spots during the day.

I patted my pocket to make sure I had the key to the collars still. My knives were in their sheaths, and I had my lock picks in another pocket. Ready to rock and roll. We headed to the water's edge and followed it toward the house we wanted, moving easily in the dark.

A tall fence ran right to the canal's edge, dividing the park from the house next door. We hung out over the canal as we swung carefully around the end of the fence. I wondered how Cerberus would manage, but he solved the problem by leaping the fence instead, clearing it with room to spare. There were no lights showing inside the house. Either they were all asleep or there was no one home. Some of these places were probably only holiday homes and not their owners' main residence, rich as they were.

The fence on the far side of the property ran right out into the water, and stood well above even Lucas's head. He cursed as he looked up at it. "I'm a wolf, not a bloody monkey."

Syl eyed the water doubtfully. Most cats hated getting

wet, and she was no exception. Sure, she could take such a long shower that she used all the hot water in our little tank in the apartment, but cold water was a no-no. "Looks like it's climb or swim."

He grumbled, but managed to scramble over with a running start. But when we arrived at the other side of the property and found an even taller fence extending out into the water, he growled and turned around.

"Where are you going?" Syl hissed.

My night vision was good, since I had connected with Cerberus to boost it. I saw him descend a set of steps onto a jetty. A small rowboat was tied up there.

He grinned back at us. "The oars are here. All aboard!"

"There could be anything in that water," Syl objected.

"That's why we're using the boat," he said patiently. "No one's going in the water."

"What if there are crocodiles?"

"Don't be ridiculous," I said. "Brenvale isn't tropical enough for crocs." Of course, there might be sharks—the canals were salt water, and I'd heard that bull sharks were occasionally sighted—but I wasn't going to mention that. For all I knew, the watershapers had figured some way to keep them out of their city. Besides, Lucas was right—we were boating, not swimming.

He held the boat steady and offered a hand to Syl. "Hop in."

"It's not very big," she said doubtfully. "What about Cerberus?"

We all turned to look at the three dogs. She was right—there was way too much dog for the size of the boat. They cocked their heads in unison and stared back, red flames dancing in the depths of their dark eyes.

"Can you handle the fences, buddy?" I asked. "You could follow us along the river bank."

PUNY FENCES, he said, which I took as a yes.

"That's settled, then. He'll follow on land."

"Good. Come on, Syl." Lucas motioned her towards the boat. She stepped onto the jetty as if she thought it would give way under her weight. "The boat's big enough for three of us. You're the smallest—hop in up the front, there."

Still she hesitated, so he swept her up in his arms and deposited her in the bow. She gave a muffled squawk and held very tightly to both sides as Lucas and I got in.

Lucas took the oars, and sculled quietly away from the jetty. The night sank down on us, cool and very dark. There was no moon, and the banks were only darker shapes in the blackness sliding past on each side. Lucas made almost no noise as he rowed, the blade of each oar cutting the water cleanly.

"This is probably close enough," I said once we had passed a few more houses. "Stop here while I check the place out."

"Good," said Syl, her voice still grumpy. "Can we get out now?"

Lucas rested on the oars for a moment, leaving the little boat to drift silently down the canal. "I'd like to get closer. I want to check out the terrain myself while you're searching inside."

"Lexi can tell you whatever you need to know," Syl said.

"She's not a hunter," he said. "She won't see what I see."

I rolled my eyes at such typical shifter prejudice, but no one noticed in the dark. "Fine," I said, before they could get into an argument. "We'll get closer."

Lucas closed the distance between us and our target in strong, easy strokes. The shadow shapers' property glowed like a beacon in the dark, the only place still lit up. Syl clung to the sides of the boat as if she were on a rollercoaster.

I shifted on my seat to balance the boat better and she gave me a sharp glance. "Sit still. You'll tip us over."

"It's perfectly safe," Lucas said, leaning into his stroke with a skill that showed this wasn't his first time in a boat. "We're not going to tip over."

It made no difference. She continued to watch the smooth, dark surface of the river with deep distrust until I directed Lucas to pull in under some overhanging willows on the far side of the river from the shadow shapers' house, beyond the range of their lights. We weren't directly opposite, but close enough for Lucas to check the place out to his heart's content.

The top floor of the house was dark, but the rest of it was well lit. Even the grounds were bright, though no one was outside. The tennis court was ablaze, and ornamental lamp posts lit a paved path that led from the lowest terrace to the tennis court and past it all the way to the boat shed and jetty. A couple of rowboats were tied up there now, not much bigger than ours.

I settled more comfortably on the hard, wooden bench and closed my eyes, sending my mind out into the night. Moths orbited each glowing lamp post, and hurled themselves at the floodlights on the tennis court. A small owl perched on the big gum closest to the house; through her eyes, I saw a swimmer cutting through the rippling waters of the elevated pool, indulging in a midnight swim. Wavering blue reflections danced over the white ceiling above the swimmer.

But I needed something inside the house. A couple of cockroaches scurried in the dark crevices below the pool, but inside was remarkably bug-free. No mice inside the walls, no cockroaches in the pantry. Ah, but *there* was something I could use—a dog.

Excellent. He was curled up on an expensive-looking leather lounge in a giant living area overlooking the rear terrace, with a diamante-studded collar around his fluffy white neck. A tiny, spoiled dog—even better. He probably had the run of the whole house. I prodded him awake and sent him pattering across the polished wooden floor.

We followed the sound of voices and clinking cutlery to a vast dining room where a long table sat twelve or fourteen people. The dog's nose quivered at the scents wafting from the plates. A woman seated at the foot of the table saw the dog and clicked her fingers invitingly at him. I refused to let him go to her; he seemed just the right size to be picked up and cuddled, and I didn't want to lose my furry spy.

Scanning the faces at the table, I felt a chill of recognition as the dog's gaze fell on Bruno's face. I'd never known his surname, but he'd been one of the shadow shapers involved with EmeryCorp and the vile Mrs Emery in Newport. It was no great surprise to find him here, seated at the head of the table. Who were these others with him? More shadow shapers? Local watershapers he was trying to persuade to the shadow shapers' cause? I hoped they all choked on their meals.

The woman clicked her fingers at the dog again. "What's the matter, baby? Are you looking for something? Have you lost your ball?"

Ha. If she only knew what I was looking for it would wipe that sickly sweet smile from her face. I guided the dog from the room and went to explore the rest of this level.

We found nothing of interest, just more luxury. Seriously, did people really need a whole cinema in their own house? On the ground floor, we found some closed doors, but the dog sniffed at the gap beneath the door, and it didn't smell as though there were any people behind them, so we moved on. There were several people busy in the kitchen, which had the same enticing smells that had so interested the dog upstairs, but none of them took any notice of him.

A spiral staircase off the kitchen led down to a basement area, and the dog trotted down on sure feet, his nails clicking on the gleaming wood. The staircase opened onto yet another lounge area. Through an archway, rows of gym machines waited in the dark, and the scent of sweat hung in the air.

Two hallways ran away from the lounge area. There was nothing to see down one of them but a closed door at the end. The space on the other side of the door smelled of petrol and hot metal, so I assumed it was the garage. That would put it roughly underneath the pool, so that seemed right.

Back we went and tried the other hallway. This seemed more promising. It offered four doors, two on each side. All were closed except the first door on the left. Light spilled from the room into the otherwise dim corridor. A man sitting at a desk looked up at the sound of the dog's claws clicking on the floor.

"Hello, boy. What are you doing down here, hey?" He reached out and I allowed the dog close enough to be patted while I checked out the room. Three big computer screens sat on the long desk, as if this was a shared work space, though only one of them was active. It showed what appeared to be a video feed of a windowless room, lit only by downlights that had been dimmed, perhaps to allow the room's occupant to sleep.

The room contained nothing but a bed. Judging by the short hair, the person in the bed was a man. He was facing the wall, so I couldn't see his face, but my heart leapt all the same. Who else would be locked in a windowless room—barely more than a cell, despite the luxury on display everywhere else in this mansion—but the person I was seeking? It was someone important, perhaps someone they even feared, given the fact they didn't even dare allow him true darkness to sleep, but they had to have someone watching him all the time. They were taking no chances with this prisoner.

I took the dog back out into the corridor and gazed at the three closed doors that remained. Behind one of these Hades lay; I was almost certain. I was so excited I almost lost my grip on the dog's mind. He sniffed at the bottom of each door. Only one smelled as though someone was in the room.

"What are you doing, you stupid dog?" the man asked, coming to the open door of his little guard station. "Get away from there."

A dull slamming of car doors turned both man and dog's

heads towards the sound. The man stayed in the doorway, but I sent the dog trotting back down the corridor toward the noise. Voices, muffled at first, then louder once the door between the garage and the house opened. Footsteps on concrete. It sounded as though several people had arrived. They brought with them a renewed smell of petrol and the faint stench of burnt rubber.

A group of men appeared, led by a familiar face. The dog whined at the surge of animosity over the link between us. Adrian. I'd hoped he'd died in the collapse of the house back in Newport, but no such luck. Here he was, still neck-deep in the shadow shapers' schemes, apparently still in Mrs Emery's good books. I was surprised I hadn't seen her yet.

"All quiet here?" Adrian asked, stopping the group when he caught sight of the guard standing in the doorway of his little office. "No trouble with the prisoner?"

"No, sir. He's been asleep since my shift started."

"Good." Adrian led the group through the lounge to the spiral staircase, no doubt off to join the party upstairs.

I'd seen enough. I released the dog and fell back into my own body.

The darkness in our little hideaway under the drooping branches of the willow was strange after the light, however dim, inside the house. Syl started as I punched the air, rocking the small boat.

"Found him!" I crowed.

"Is he hurt?" Syl asked, frowning at me for the boat-rocking.

That sobered me a little. Maybe that was why he'd lain so still. "I don't know. Couldn't tell from the look I got."

"Did you get a look at the exits?" Lucas asked. "What's the plan?"

"He's down on the basement level. One exit through the garage, another up a spiral staircase into the kitchen. It's all underground, so no windows."

Lucas looked thoughtful. "That's a nuisance. Still, we expected as much. How many in the house?"

"At the moment, maybe twenty. Looks like a late dinner party going on."

"We could use that as cover—go in while they're distracted."

I shook my head. "No, the kitchen's full of staff. Better to wait until most of them have gone home. We've got all night."

"Good," Syl said. "Does that mean we can get off this stupid river and back onto dry land?"

"Sure. Let's head over to Cerberus and work out exactly what we're doing." I couldn't see him, but the three red sparks of his life force stood out to my mind's sight, lurking in the darkness of the property next to the shadow shapers' house.

Lucas nodded, and used an oar against the bank to push

the boat out from under the hanging branches. The leaves parted like a veil, sliding across our heads and shoulders in a gentle caress as we left the shelter of the willow tree.

None of us spoke as the boat glided over the dark water toward the far bank, all watching the brightly lit house. We were nearly halfway across when the boat jarred as we bumped against something. Syl half-swallowed a shriek. "What was that?"

Lucas peered into the dark, but even his shifter vision wasn't up to the task. "Don't know. Probably just a bit of floating wood."

In the darkness, I could make out the glimmer of Syl's pale arms, reaching out to take a better grip on the sides of the boat.

Another bump jarred us, and even I grabbed hold of the seat. What the hell? It felt as though we'd run into something much bigger than a piece of wood.

The next thing I knew, I was flung into the air as the stern of the boat flew up out of the water. It happened so quickly I didn't even get a chance to take a breath before I was underwater.

The water was freezing, and pitch black. I struggled, weighed down by my clothes and heavy boots. Hoping I had the right direction, I kicked out hard for the surface, desperate for air. The darkness was so impenetrable that Syl could have been right next to me and I wouldn't have seen her. My head broke the surface and I gulped in a great relieved breath.

And then a hand closed around my ankle and pulled me back under.

11

I'm not ashamed to say I panicked. It was dark and I couldn't see a thing. I nearly lost the breath I'd just sucked in from the shock of feeling something grab me, and I kicked out in terror with my free foot. I forgot Lucas and Syl in the sheer primal terror of near-drowning. I needed air! Which way was up? I thrashed and kicked against whatever had my leg, frantic.

My lungs burned with the need for air. I jack-knifed, trying to reach the knife in my boot, but more hands took my arms, dragging me down. I couldn't hold out much longer. My chest convulsed as I fought the reflex that insisted I open my mouth and take a breath.

My head banged against something hard, and the last of my air rushed from my mouth in a stream of bubbles. But before I could breathe in a lungful of water, the hands fell away and the water itself convulsed, hurling me skyward.

I broke the surface, gasping and retching. Sweet air had never felt so good as I filled my aching lungs.

"There you go," said a voice. "Grab on, that's a good girl."

My blindly reaching hand closed on a smooth metal bar. I looked up, straight into a spotlight that dazzled my vision, and hung there in the cold water, blinking. Something breached the surface an arm's length away, gasping and heaving in air as I'd just done. As my vision cleared, I realised it was Lucas.

Suddenly I looked around, panic churning in my gut. "Where's Syl?"

"I'm here." A figure loomed above me; a black silhouette against the glare of the spotlight. She was on a boat, a large boat, and I was holding onto the ladder hanging over the back of it.

Where the hell had a boat this size come from without us noticing it before? Whatever. I wasn't about to look a gift boat in the mouth, that was for sure. Plus, I had a feeling that the boat's owner had somehow driven away the owners of the hands who had threatened to drag me down to death. I gripped the rungs of the ladder with both hands and hauled myself up out of the water, eager to be out of their reach.

Hands reached out again, but this time, they were helping. Syl got a grip on one arm and the strange man grabbed a handful of my wet shirt at the back. Together, they pulled me over the transom and onto the deck. I sank down onto the deck, my knees unaccountably weak. There was nothing like a near-drowning to knock the stuffing out of a girl.

"You all right there?" the man asked, bending over to wrap a thick blanket around my trembling shoulders. His left arm was covered in a complicated tattoo of Celtic knots that tangled all the way to his shoulder. It left my own tiny archer tattoo for dead.

Now that the spotlight was no longer shining in my eyes, I got my first good look at the rest of him. He was young, mid to late twenties. His brown, shoulder-length hair had blonde streaks bleached into it by the sun, and his skin was deeply tanned. He looked like he should be a lifeguard on some sun-soaked beach, not cruising up a dark canal in the middle of the night.

Lucas's wet head appeared at the top of the ladder and he joined me on the deck, shaking himself like a dog, flinging drops of water over all of us.

"Welcome aboard," the man said with a cheery grin. "You're quite safe now."

Lucas eyed him, not quite so cheerfully. I got the impression that werewolves didn't like unexpected dunkings any more than cats did. "Who are you?"

"You can call me Mac."

Hmm. I wiped my face with the edge of the blanket and clambered shakily to my feet. I felt at a disadvantage staring up at him like a little kid. He hadn't actually said his name was Mac, only that we could call him that.

"What just happened?" I asked.

Mac handed Lucas a blanket. He used it like a towel, and rubbed himself briskly down. Syl was already wrapped up in one, looking small and bedraggled. I pulled mine a little tighter around myself; the night air was cold when you were wet. I wrung my hair out onto the deck, trying to disguise the shaking of my hands.

"Looked like you capsized," Mac said.

"We didn't. Something—or someone—threw us into the water. And then tried to drown us." I couldn't keep the note of outrage from my voice.

Mac spread his hands in a helpless gesture. "The local Merrow aren't very friendly sometimes."

"Not very friendly?" Lucas burst out. "The bastards tried to kill us."

"Lucky I was here, then." Mac smiled, and crow's feet appeared at the corners of his eyes. Suddenly, he looked a lot older than I'd first thought.

"Lucky," I agreed, suddenly cautious. He hadn't been anywhere near us before the Merrow attacked; I was positive. How had he got there so fast, and where had he come from? He was obviously some kind of watershaper.

That surge I'd felt as the water lifted me up toward the surface would have given that away, even without his apparent ability to snatch us from the hands of the Merrow.

I'd never met a Merrow before, although I'd heard of them. They weren't common in the southern waters. They were an odd kind of shifter in that, unlike most shifters, they didn't completely transform into their animal shape. Their top half remained human while their bottom half turned fish. They had a bad reputation as ship wreckers and drowners of men. Guess we'd just had that one confirmed. I wondered what a pod of them were doing here in Sanctuary Point, and whether they were connected to the shadow shapers. Maybe they were the reason there was no apparent security on the canal side of the property—they were the security.

For that matter, was our new friend in league with the shadow shapers? But if so, why would he have saved us? He might as well have let the Merrow drown us, since the job had nearly been finished anyway. As usual, I had way more questions than answers.

"How did you drive the Merrow away?"

Mac turned off the powerful spotlight now that we were all safely aboard. It was a relief—I'd felt like I was on a stage, exposed for anyone out there in the dark to see. It also meant I could no longer see the violently pink flowers all over his lurid shirt so clearly, which was no bad thing.

The guy wouldn't be winning any fashion awards with his wardrobe choices. He grinned at me. "I can be very persuasive when I want to. It's my charming personality, you see."

"Really?" If Apollo had said that, I would have branded him a wanker, but this guy's grin was so infectious I couldn't help smiling back.

"Really. I could talk a werewolf into becoming a vegetarian."

Lucas snorted. I wondered if Mac could tell that Lucas was a wolf, or if it had been a random remark. My guess was the former. I got the feeling there was a lot going on under the surface of Mr Sunny Side Up.

"Can I drop you folks off somewhere?" he asked.

"Do you live locally?" I asked.

"Here and there." The twinkle in his eye said he was enjoying my frustration at his evasiveness.

"We're very lucky you were here right when we needed you," Syl said, making big eyes at him. From the corner of my eye, I saw Lucas bristle. I could have told him not to worry; Syl was only fishing for information. "Are you a watershaper?"

"Something like that," Mac agreed cheerfully, not swayed by her flattery. He was awfully tight-lipped for someone whose manner appeared so open. My gratitude at being saved from a watery death began to be replaced by an eagerness to get away. He was charming, but we didn't need any charming shapers throwing a spanner in our plans.

"Just drop us anywhere over there," I said, indicating the dark property where Cerberus was waiting. "We can find our own way home."

Two could play at being evasive.

"What were you doing out here so late anyway?" he asked, as the boat began to move across the dark canal. There was no steering wheel or engine, and it was certainly too big to pole or row. One of those watershaper waves appeared at the stern, pushing the boat along, though he uttered no command and made no obvious move. He must have been controlling it with his mind. Impressive.

"Fishing," I said, daring him to challenge me.

"You'll find the fish bite better at dawn and dusk," he said, as if he believed me, though I was quite sure he didn't.

"I'll remember that next time."

He pulled the boat in at the dark jetty. I searched the blackness under the trees for red, glowing eyes, but thankfully, the hellhound remained hidden.

"I heard there were some new folk in town," he said, "though my informant ended up taking an unexpected swim in the canal."

I didn't dare look at Lucas, though I could feel him tense at my side. Ready to tear this guy's throat out if he had to. "I hope he didn't have any trouble with the Merrow."

"No, he was fine, and the Merrow have gone off to consider the wisdom of their life choices." He smiled at me, his eyes as dark as the pitch-black waters of the canal, and just as hard to see what was going on beneath the surface. "You know, not everyone you meet is an enemy."

"It's safer to assume that everyone is. That way you don't get any nasty surprises." I took off my blanket and handed it to him. "Thank you for your help."

My wet clothes were plastered to my body. Without the blanket, goosebumps rose on my bare arms.

"You look cold." He didn't move or say anything else, but the water evaporated from my clothes. In a moment, I was as dry as if I'd never fallen into the canal. He nodded in satisfaction. "That's better."

I stared. This guy had some serious power. Lucas and Syl removed their blankets, too, and they were also dry underneath. That would make Syl happy, at least. Lucas helped her onto the jetty. I patted my pocket, checking reflexively for the key before I joined them.

"Oh, shit."

"What's wrong?" Lucas turned back, instantly ready to defend me, but there was nothing he could do about this.

I could feel the blood draining from my face. We were so screwed. Our whole plan hinged on that key. "The key's gone. It must have fallen out of my pocket when I went into the water."

"Oh, no." Syl's hands flew to her mouth.

"Lost something?" Mac asked.

I nodded, my mind numb. What would we *do*? There was no more star-metal to make another. Hades would be trapped in that collar forever, if we could even break him out of the shadow shapers' house. Our escape plan had depended on him being at full strength. Frantically, I cast my mind into the water, searching for fish I could use to find the key, but the water was strangely free of aquatic life. The Merrow must have frightened them all away.

"A key. I needed it for—for my friend."

"Friends are important." He turned and looked out over the dark canal. After a moment, he said, "Is it a dull silver colour?"

"Yes." I stared at him, hardly daring to hope.

A column of water erupted beside the boat. Mac reached into it. Was that—?

It was. He held out his hand. The key lay in his palm, undamaged by its sojourn in the depths. I took it from him almost reverently. Who *was* this guy?

"Thank you," I whispered.

"Give my regards to your friend," he said.

I nodded, unable to speak, and stepped off the boat. He raised a hand in farewell as the boat turned silently away from the jetty.

"What did you make of him?" I asked, watching until

the boat disappeared into the dark. My mind was still blown by what had just happened.

"Fishy as all hell," Lucas growled. "Had he been watching us? He just came out of nowhere."

"Maybe he set those Merrow on us," Syl said.

"So he could rescue us and make a big fellow of himself?" I shook my head. That didn't feel right. Not only had he saved our lives, but he'd retrieved the precious key as well. "What would be the point of that? Maybe he was watching the shadow shapers himself."

"Maybe." That thought seemed to cheer her. "And he did get the key back. Just tell me that I don't have to get back into a boat for the rest of the night."

"Damn. There goes plan A."

She growled and shoved me in the shoulder. "Don't mess with me, girl."

Cerberus appeared out of the dark, tongues lolling out in happy greeting.

"You'll like plan B, though," I told her. "I thought we'd swim up the river disguised as Merrow."

"You think you're such a comedian." She stepped off the jetty, moving away from the hated water. "Don't give up your day job."

12

Two hours later, a small black cat strolled along the top of the wall that separated the shadow shapers' property from its neighbour as if she owned it. Lucas and I, plus the three Cerberuses—Cerberi?—waited in the darkness on the other side of the wall. A couple of cars had left the mansion an hour ago and the people who remained had gone to their rooms on the top floor.

Do you see anyone? I asked Syl.

Nope. No lights on anywhere inside the house. Just out here.

The yard was still brightly lit, the spotlights blazing down on the tennis court as if they were about to play a tournament there. That posed something of a problem. I slid into Syl's mind and looked out of her eyes.

That balcony door up on the left-hand side looks good. There were five smaller balconies on the top level of the massive house, all with sliding doors leading inside. Probably bedrooms. It looked as though somebody liked plenty of fresh air while they slept, because they'd left their balcony door open. All we had to do was climb up to it and, hey, presto—instant access.

As long as you can get to it without being caught on camera.

Yes, that was the problem. Four cameras mounted high up on the sides of the house were probably never even noticed by the guests, but they were a serious headache for us.

"This place has more security than the bloody Ruby Palace," I complained to Lucas. There, I'd summoned cockroaches to swarm the lenses of a couple of cameras for the moment's cover I'd needed. But I couldn't pull that stunt again. Here, the shadow shapers would be expecting a rescue attempt. If four camera feeds went out at once, all hell would break loose.

Lucas crouched beside me in the shadow of the wall. "Maybe no one's monitoring the cameras at this time of night. They might all be in bed."

They might be, but I couldn't afford to risk it. I sent my mind out in search of the bright spark that was the little dog I'd used earlier. He was asleep, curled up on the foot of someone's bed, so I prodded him awake. Fortunately, the bedroom door wasn't closed. He hopped down onto the thick carpet and trotted out into the hallway at my direction, and we hurried through the dark house together.

On the next floor down the living areas, with their huge glass walls open to the floodlit yard, were bright, their glittering elegance cold and empty, now, without people. We easily found our way through the kitchen to the small spiral staircase that led down to the basement area. The tiny clicks of the dog's claws on the marble floor were the only sound in the stillness.

At the bottom of the stairs, the lounge area and the gym were dark, but light spilled in a bright rectangle across the hallway from the open door of the guard room. Damn. It had been too much to hope that there would be no one on duty in the wee hours of the morning. The shadow shapers knew that Hades had friends, and we wouldn't let them have him without a fight. At least they hadn't managed to get their hands on the Helm. Safe back in the underworld with Hephaistos, it was the only thing keeping Hades alive.

I paused the dog in the doorway. The man on duty was slouched in his chair, feet up on the long desk, his phone in his hand. He was scrolling through something on the phone, but every few seconds his gaze would flick to the monitors, checking that nothing had changed. Did we have time to sprint from the wall to the side of the house in those moments of inattention?

Maybe, but to then climb up to the balcony? Scroll,

scroll, flick. I counted the seconds. Scroll, scroll, flick. Damn. Either he was too diligent, or his feed wasn't interesting enough. I needed his girlfriend to send him nudes, or something equally distracting.

Outside, I stood up. "Get ready," I said to Lucas.

Are we moving? Syl asked, peering down at me from the top of the wall. *What's the plan?*

You stay here and keep watch. I said. *Lucas and I are going in. And make sure you don't get distracted this time.* I didn't want a repeat of the disaster with Rosie and Winston and the "trapped cat". We wouldn't be able to talk our way out of trouble this time.

You said there was a secret compartment! What was I supposed to do?

You were supposed to stay on watch. But don't worry, if I find any secret compartments this time, you'll be the last person I tell.

She stalked away along the wall with a grumpy flick of her tail. Lucas waited patiently beside me, his eyes trained on my face.

"We don't have a big window," I told him. Cerberus listened, too, red eyes unblinking, ears pricked. "There's a guy watching the camera feed, and I'm going to try distracting him with the dog. When I say 'go', we have to move."

SAVE MASTER NOW? Cerberus asked, the tips of his tails twitching in the smallest of wags.

Should I get him to re-form into one giant hellhound again? Maybe once we were in. I wasn't sure his massive bulk would fit through that door on the balcony. *Yes. Stay close.*

I turned my attention to the little white dog inside. The guard hadn't noticed him yet. His feet were still on the desk, the chair swivelled away from the door.

Okay, time to get this party started. I sent the dog charging down the hall toward Hades' room, barking his little fluffy head off. The guard's feet thudded to the floor.

"Go!" I said to Lucas.

He boosted me up, and I caught the top of the wall and scrambled over, dropping to the soft grass on the other side. In a moment, he was beside me. The three Cerberi sailed over the wall as if it wasn't even there, and led the way toward the house.

I pounded along in their wake, heart pumping. We were so exposed. All it would take was for one person to look out a window …

Inside, the guard flicked on the hallway light. "What the hell are you fussing about, dog? What are you barking at?" He carried a gun, and looked alert but not threatening. "Shut up before you wake the whole house."

I thought he—and we—were probably safe enough in that regard. At least two levels of the house separated the subterranean hallway from any of the bedrooms. Most of the sleepers wouldn't be disturbed by the dog's high-pitched barking.

We ran up onto the terrace and paused beneath the balcony with the open door. It was higher than the wall we'd just climbed, and there were no handy trees—not even a drainpipe. Not that they usually worked, despite all the books I'd read where people managed to shin up a conveniently placed drainpipe as easily as if it were a ladder and not a smooth pipe that was far more likely to pull away from the wall and dump you on your arse. Noisily.

One of the Cerberi took a running start and leapt into the air, his front paws catching the railing above with a thud that sounded horribly loud in the still night. My heart leapt into my mouth as I watched his back feet scrabbling against empty air, fighting to pull himself up.

Stand there and don't move, I ordered the nearest Cerberus, then threw myself on his back, feeling like a circus performer as I struggled to find my feet. He kept as still as he could, considering the urgency thrumming through his body. I could feel it through our link. He wanted nothing more than to rend his way through our enemies to Hades' side. But despite his stillness and the broadness of his back, I wobbled like a kid trying to stand on a surfboard for the first time. I managed to grab hold of the balcony railing above me seconds before I lost my balance completely and ended up flat on my back on the flagstones.

The Cerberus above me nosed the balcony door open.

Wait! I shot at him. *Wait for the rest of us.*

He didn't bother replying, just shouldered his way through the door. Dammit. I hauled myself up onto the balcony, trying to force him to stop, but with my attention divided between him and what was going on downstairs, I couldn't summon enough power to compel him.

It all happened so quickly. One minute, I was clambering over the railing, Lucas by my side, watching the first Cerberus's hindquarters disappearing into the dark house while another nearly shoved me back over the railing in his eagerness to join the first. The next minute, there was an almighty boom and a blinding flash of light. I threw my arms up to shield my face. Something pierced my leg, my shoulder, my arm. My ears rang, and I was only dimly aware of Lucas's big body between me and the blast.

The balcony groaned, and one side dropped with a jolt that threw me from my feet. I landed on something large and warm. Cerberus. He wasn't moving. I turned my head, forcing myself to my hands and knees. What was happening?

Lucas knelt beside me, shaking his head as if to clear it. He was covered in blood, and pieces of glass stuck out of him as if he were a werewolf pincushion. Something warm trickled down my arm. Blood. A jagged piece of glass stuck out of my shoulder. Broken glass lay everywhere, blasted out of the balcony door. Cerberus's black fur sparkled as if a thousand diamonds had been scattered over him. His chest rose and fell, but otherwise, he was still.

I staggered to my feet, picking glass off me, surveying the gaping hole that led into the house.

Holy crap, are you all right? Syl's panicked voice sounded in my head. *What the hell was that?*

Bomb.

Inside was a war zone. It may have been a bedroom once, but there was no furniture left, only pieces of kindling that might once have been a bed. Fire smouldered sluggishly among the ruins.

They had known we would come. That balcony door, so conveniently left open—why had I not seen it for the trap it was? Rage burned within me. I was a fool. We had walked straight into it.

On the far side of the room, a black shape lay, thrown against the wall like a discarded toy. I stepped inside.

"What are you doing?" Lucas hissed. "We've got to get out of here."

I ignored him.

Lexi, no! Syl shouted. *You'll be caught! Come on!*

I ignored her, too, sending my mind out toward the huddled shape. The red fire of his life force flickered, barely more than a spark. Shouts of alarm sounded through the house. The guard downstairs pounded up the stairs, the little white dog at his heels.

I dropped to my knees at Cerberus's side. One of his front legs had been severed, and black blood pulsed sluggishly from the stump. Half of his body was raw flesh, his fur burned away in the blast. Through a gaping hole in his side, I could see the glistening coils of intestines—and blood, blood everywhere. I reached out a hand, but there was nowhere I could touch him that wouldn't add to his agony. My hand fell limply back to my lap.

"We have to leave him." Lucas tugged insistently at my arm. His words sounded very far away, lost to the ringing in my ears.

I snatched my arm away. "I don't understand. He's a hellhound. He took on all those shadow shapers without a scratch." Back in Newport, nothing could touch him. How could he be lying here like this?

Lucas bent over, hugging an arm around his middle. He looked as though someone had poured a bucket of blood over his head. "Lexi, we only have a moment. We've got to get out while we still can. There's nothing you can do for him. The others are both lying down like someone just flipped the off switch. We have to leave them."

I glanced over my shoulder to the balcony, where the second Cerberus lay as still as death, though he was nowhere near as wounded as this one. The third hadn't even made it to the balcony—and yet he had collapsed, too?

"Please, Lexi," Lucas said, catching at my arm again. His

eyes were yellowing, the wolf very close to the surface. "I have to change. I need the wolf to deal with this much damage. But I don't want to leave you."

Running feet in the corridor. Lucas gazed at me imploringly, his eyes blazing golden. We were almost out of time. I sighed, a great shuddering breath, and chased after that dying red spark deep within the wreck of Cerberus's body. Lucas's hand fell away from my arm, and I was dimly aware of him convulsing by my side. But I was focused on that spark, gathering it, folding it protectively into myself. If I could just hold onto it long enough to reunite it with its other two parts, perhaps he could be made whole again. United, they had been invincible. Perhaps it was only because they'd been separated that they were vulnerable.

The spark flickered, dangerously close to going out. A sob shuddered through me, but I clung to it with fierce determination, pushing some of my own life force at it. I was *not* going to lose him. With another part of my mind, I reached out, searching for the other two parts of him. Their red fires should be burning much brighter, easy to find. Hell, I could see one of the Cerberi right there on the balcony. His life force glowed, but I couldn't reach it. It was as if it was on the other side of a pane of glass. I pushed against the barrier, but nothing happened.

Fur brushed against me—Lucas had shifted. His wolf

stretched out, panting, at my side, his life force a vivid glow next to me. I laid a hand on his warm flank and pushed again with my mind, shoving the tiny spark of Cerberus's life force toward that other red light, so tantalisingly close on the other side of the barrier. My head pounded with effort and my sight dimmed, but I kept pushing.

Cerberus! I begged. *Let me in!*

But there was no response, and the barrier wouldn't fall. Suddenly, the room was full of people, but I could barely see, my consciousness slipping away. Cerberus's tiny spark was slipping from my grasp, too. No! I couldn't lose him. There was only one thing left to try. I clenched my fist in the werewolf's fur. With my last remaining strength, I shoved the flickering spark at the bright glow of the werewolf beside me. Then I face-planted in his fur as blackness descended.

13

When I woke, my head throbbed as though someone in hobnailed boots was tap-dancing on the inside of my skull. Blearily, I blinked up at an unfamiliar ceiling, lit by a single globe. A small red light blinked back—a camera, watching my every move. I sat up, holding my head as if it might fall off if I moved too quickly. God, it hurt. Had I given myself some kind of magical injury in my attempts to reach Cerberus?

Something rattled as my feet hit the floor. In my bleary state, it took me way longer than it should have to realise that the something was a chain, and it was attached to my ankle. The other end of the chain was bolted to the bedframe. The bastards. I showed the camera my middle finger.

On the floor lay the two uninjured Cerberi, also chained. Their chains attached to a giant metal ring in the floor. If Jake were here, he would have made short work of those chains. I sighed. We could have used some of that metalshaping magic of his. But if he had been here, they would have collared him with one of their magic-blocking collars, and he would have been in the same boat as Hades, cut off from his powers.

My hand leapt to my throat in sudden fear, but I found only skin. Either they didn't have enough collars to go around, or they didn't find my power to control animals threatening enough to warrant a collar. That was something, at least. It meant I could still talk to Syl, and to Lucas, too, if he were still in werewolf form. They didn't know I could do that, and we had few enough advantages over them.

I nudged the nearest Cerberus with my foot, but got no response. They were both breathing, their massive chests rising and falling in a regular rhythm, but it was clearly no ordinary sleep. The shadow shapers probably hadn't even needed to chain them. It didn't look as though they'd be going anywhere any time soon. I pushed at the bright red glow of their life force—or tried to, at least—but that barrier still held me out.

There was nothing else in the cell. No food or water, no furniture but the bed, not even a blanket. Nothing but the red eye of the camera glaring down at me. Too bad if I wanted to go to the toilet, I guess.

Both my knife sheaths were empty. No surprises there. I felt the pocket where the all-important key to the collars had been. Naturally, that was empty, too. I closed my eyes as despair washed over me. They'd left me nothing.

Except Syl. The fact that she wasn't in here with me gave me hope that she'd escaped capture. *Syl? Where are you?*

Even sending my mind out questing for her familiar life spark intensified the pounding in my head. The answer came back at full volume, and I winced.

Oh, thank God! You're alive! I've been calling you for ages. When I saw you drop like that I thought you were dead.

I cradled my throbbing head in my hands. *I'm not that easy to kill. Ages? What time is it?*

How would I know? Cats don't wear bloody wristwatches. Well, that sounded more like the Syl we all knew and loved. *It might be an hour since you went in.*

Okay, so maybe three o'clock in the morning, then. *Where are you?*

On the roof. I ran in to help when the bomb went off, but I couldn't get to you before the shadow shapers did. And you were all just lying there like you were dead—I couldn't think what to do. Her mental tone was getting shrill. We must have scared the crap out of her. *I thought if I made it up here without anyone seeing me, I could keep an eye on things and maybe figure something out.*

That was good thinking, I said, trying to massage the

pain out of my pounding head so I could think, too. Syl being free gave us an advantage, but only if we could come up with a plan.

Where are you? she asked. *Are you all right?*

All right-ish. I'm in the basement. Feel like shit but nothing's broken, just a few cuts. At least someone had pulled all the shards of glass out of me before they chained me up. *Two of the Cerberi are with me.* I paused, watching the rise and fall of those big chests, feeling a terrible guilt that there were only two bodies lying on the floor instead of three. *He—he's not in good shape.*

What happened? One minute you were on the balcony and the next thing there was this big explosion.

I filled her in on what I'd pieced together—that one of the Cerberi, running ahead, had set off a bomb that must have been meant for me. They knew I would come for Hades. The Merrow had probably told them there'd been three people in a boat watching the house, casing the joint. So they'd prepared a little surprise welcome, and caught a third of a hellhound in their trap instead. The other two-thirds were now in some kind of magical coma. Because the other part of their threesome had died? But he wasn't truly dead. At least, I hoped not. I'd shoved that little spark of life into Lucas for safekeeping.

Where's Lucas? Syl asked, as if she'd read my mind. *Is he safe?*

Good question. I blamed my pounding headache for the fact that I hadn't wondered that already. My brain felt like it was mired in molasses. *Come on, Lexi, get it together.* People were relying on me here. I couldn't afford to be off my game.

Last time I'd seen him, he'd been in werewolf form, forced to change by his injuries. Shifters' human forms couldn't cope as well with injury as their animal ones could. He must have been hurt pretty badly to force an involuntary change. Something else to feel guilty about— he'd been in front of me, partly shielding me from the blast with his body. At least he should heal quickly in wolf form.

I cast my mind out, and found his bright spark straight away, very close. He was asleep, so I prodded him awake, and a peek out of his eyes confirmed my suspicions. He lay on the floor, and a chain clinked as he moved his head. He was tethered to a bolt in the floor, the same as the two Cerberi in my room. On a bed similar to mine, a familiar figure sat, watching him patiently—a short, older man, perhaps sixty years old, thickening through the body. Hades. His blue eyes, bright in his weathered brown face, were fixed on Lucas. He'd probably been waiting for the wolf to wake up. His bed had blankets, presumably because he'd been a "guest" a little longer than the rest of us. The shadow shapers probably figured I wasn't worth dirtying a blanket for.

Hey, it's Lexi. Are you all right? I asked the werewolf, projecting my words gently into his mind.

He took the appearance of a disembodied voice surprisingly well. Perhaps he remembered the story of how I'd snuck into Holly's wolf mind to calm her while she was giving birth. *I'm still a bit tender, but pretty good.* He looked all around the small room he shared with Hades, ignoring the god for the moment. *Where are you?*

Just across the hallway from you. The other two Cerberi are with me.

Are they alive?

Yes, but they won't wake up. I could still see the tiny red spark of the missing Cerberus's essence flickering deep inside Lucas's own white light, sheltering in the glow of his life force. *It's like they've gone offline without their other part.*

I wanted to ask Lucas if he felt odd, but then I'd have to admit why I was asking and what I'd done. It was probably weird enough for him to be talking to someone inside his own head without mentioning that he was also harbouring a piece of hellhound. If I could just figure out a way to get that piece back to its rightful owner, our troubles could be over—or at least alleviated. I was pretty sure those chains wouldn't stop Cerberus if he was firing on all cylinders again.

I'm locked up with some old guy, Lucas said. *I'm guessing that's Hades?*

Yep. That's him. Are you up to turning human yet? Tell him what's happened, and that we've come to save him.

That part doesn't seem to be working out so well, he said.

We'll figure something out. I tried to sound confident, but I don't think he was fooled. Here we were, chained in our separate rooms, with not a weapon or a magic power between us. Well, I had my power, but the shadow shapers had made sure I had no options for using it. The only animal inside the house was the little fluffy white dog—except for Cerberus, of course, but he was well and truly out of commission for now. I had a feeling it would take a god's power to put him back together. But before Hades could regain access to his power, we had to get back the damn key that the shadow shapers had taken from me. There'd be no removing the collar without it. *Syl is still free.*

Good. The relief in his voice was palpable. *Maybe she can call Winston and get Apollo to help.*

Maybe. If Apollo wouldn't help before, it seemed highly unlikely that he would now, with all of us caught. That could be a last resort if I couldn't come up with a better plan. *Why don't you bring Hades up to speed. He might have some ideas. Tell him I said hi.*

Will do.

I turned my attention back to Syl. *Found Lucas. He's okay.* I didn't mention that he had part of a hellhound inside him. That went under the heading of "things Syl didn't need to know about".

I knew he would be, she said, all fake bravado, but I knew her well enough to know she'd been near-panicked about her favourite werewolf. *Wolves are hard to kill.*

Yeah. Hopefully the rest of us were, too. Footsteps sounded in the hall outside; at least two people, maybe three. I expected them to stop at the guard station next to Hades' room, but they continued to my door, followed by the sound of a key in the lock. *Gotta go,* I said to Syl. *Looks like I've got company.*

At this time of night? Maybe they're bringing you munchies.

I'd prefer headache tablets. I eyed the door as it swung open, my stomach tightening with nerves. Whoever was at my door, I doubted I would enjoy their visit.

14

"Well, that's a blast from the past," I said. "I didn't expect to see you again."

"Nor I you." Adrian stood in the doorway, looking disappointingly well for someone who'd been inside a collapsing house last time I'd seen him.

Despite it being sometime after three in the morning, his dark hair was still sleekly gelled back from his forehead. He'd probably been waiting for his trap to be triggered rather than sleeping. There was a small red stain on his white shirt, near the breast pocket, but unfortunately it looked more like red wine than blood. Must have been a good dinner party. "I could hardly believe it when Bruno told me it was you. I had to come and see for myself."

I remained seated on the bed, leaning back against the wall, trying to look casual. "What are you lot doing in a shaper city? You were so gung-ho about human rights last time I saw you, this is the last place I would have expected to find you. How are all those downtrodden humans back in Newport managing without you?"

The keys to the cell were still in his hand as he shut the door. Did they also unlock the chain around my ankle? Perhaps if I goaded him, he'd come close enough that we could find out. I certainly wouldn't be making any surprise attacks with that chain weighing me down.

He smiled as he closed the door and put the keys in his pocket. The crow's feet around his eyes crinkled in the most disarming way when he smiled, which just went to show you could never judge a book by its cover. It sickened me, now, that I had once thought we could be friends. "Where else to hunt shaper gods than in shaper cities?"

"Did many of your cockroach friends manage to scuttle to safety after our last meeting?"

"You always like to go straight on the attack, don't you? You killed quite a few of my friends, you know."

"You need better friends."

"I admire your bravado, if not your politics."

"What can I say? I'm skilled."

"You certainly are. I wish you hadn't chosen the wrong side in this battle. You could have been a great asset for us."

I shrugged. "I'm not really a team player. I like to do things my way."

He folded his arms across his chest and leaned back

against the door. Damn. It didn't look as though he intended to come any closer. "Your way has brought you to this." He nodded at the chain around my ankle. "Not working out so well for you anymore, is it?"

"At least the bed's comfy." I bounced a little on the mattress to prove my point. "Although I think you could have tried harder with the blankets. The minimalist look is nice and all, but you've probably taken it a little too far."

He didn't reply, just watched me, a little smile playing at the corners of his mouth. A smug, self-satisfied kind of smile. Supremely relaxed, he leaned against the door looking as though he was enjoying every minute of this. Obviously, my goading skills needed work.

"So, how's Mrs E enjoying life with only one arm? Having any trouble wiping her arse when she goes to the toilet, or do you do that for her?"

The annoying smirk didn't budge. It was starting to make me nervous. That was an A-grade *I know something you don't know* kind of a smirk.

"Mrs Emery is coping remarkably well. Of course, she has a state-of-the-art prosthetic. You can hardly tell it isn't her own arm."

"Already? She must be a fast healer."

"She's the strongest of us."

"Right. Silly me. All those stolen powers of yours come in handy for more than just murdering people, I guess."

"You can see her for yourself soon enough. She'll be here in the morning."

Yay. I could hardly wait.

"She's very keen to have a chat with you," he continued. "She was very surprised when I told her about this."

He pulled something from his breast pocket, something that shone with a familiar pewter gleam. It was the key that unlocked Mrs Emery's vile collars, the one that Brontes had made on the banks of the River Styx after I'd freed him from Tartarus. The one that Mac had fished out of the canal for me. The one this bastard had stolen from my pocket—and now, he'd come here to gloat about it. He held it up to the light, turning it back and forth admiringly. "It's a lovely piece of work, isn't it? Mrs Emery thought there was only one in existence. She's dying to know where you found this."

She could die with my blessing, because I wouldn't be telling her anything. I opened my eyes wide in mock innocence. "That old thing? I just had it lying around somewhere."

"Well, it's nice to have a spare. I'm sure you'll tell us eventually."

"I wouldn't hold my breath if I were you."

The smirk widened into a grin. "I think you'll find Mrs Emery can be very persuasive. You'll be begging to tell her everything you know by the time she's finished with you."

"Oh, please. You've been watching too much TV. Did you get those lines from a B-grade movie?"

He slipped the key back into his pocket, his mouth a thin line. "You talk tough, but there are no animals here for you to use except Snowy, and I really doubt a lapdog will be your salvation, particularly as we've locked him up. You're out of tricks, and out of time. In the end, we'll get what we want. *Everything* we want." He gazed down at Cerberus, collapsed all over the floor, and the smirk returned. "I must thank you for bringing this fellow along. He's definitely no lapdog. Such a prize."

The way he referred to Cerberus set alarm bells ringing in my head. To all intents and purposes, there were two dogs lying on the floor. Identical dogs, yes, but as far as anyone could see, they were completely separate. But calling them "this fellow" made it sound as if he knew they were really part of the same creature.

"No, they're a little too big for lapdogs," I said. "Shame you killed their brother with that cowardly trap."

"It's ironic, really," he said, ignoring my words. "You came all this way to free Hades, and you came so close. You even had the key you needed to unlock the collar and release his powers. And instead you've delivered the means of his destruction. We couldn't have asked for more if we'd planned it ourselves."

His eyes gleamed as he met my alarmed gaze. What was

he talking about? Hades was safe until they got their hands on his avatar, and that was never going to happen. The Helm was back in the underworld, being guarded by Hephaistos, the dead god of metalshaping. Did they think Hephaistos would trade it to save Cerberus's life? They had rocks in their head if so. No hellhound was worth the Lord of the Underworld's life, even if he was a treasured pet.

"Catching a couple of dogs doesn't get you the Helm."

He frowned in puzzlement. "What Helm? What are you talking about?"

We stared at each other for a long moment, him confused, me furious and frightened and trying hard not to show it.

And then he burst out laughing. He laughed and laughed, bent over with his hands on his knees. He laughed until tears ran from his eyes and, all the while, a cold terror crept upward from my gut into my chest, squeezing my lungs with an icy fist. When he finally stopped laughing, I was trembling, no longer able to offer even a pretence of casualness, my fists squeezing the edge of the mattress hard. Something dark and dreadful hung over my head. I could *feel* it there, waiting to drop and bury me.

"You don't know, do you?" His mouth twitched again as he fought off another fit of laughter. He shook his head. "You really don't know."

Tell me, then, you bastard. The suspense was killing me.

He waved his hand at Cerberus. "This is a surprise, of course. No one knew he could split into separate beings like this. Though perhaps not so separate after all, I suppose, considering the effect the death of one part has had on the others." He frowned. "I hope that doesn't mean we've lost any of the avatar's power. If we'd known he was with you, we might have reconsidered the bomb. Still, this is such a windfall, we shouldn't really be ungrateful, should we?"

He smiled at me, but I could only stare back at him, those words repeating over and over in my head: *the avatar's power*. Gods above, what was he saying? The Helm was Hades' avatar; even Apollo thought so.

"I can't believe you didn't …" He shook his head again, still smiling. "I can't wait to tell Mrs Emery."

"Tell her what, arsehole?"

"That Hades' would-be rescuers delivered his avatar right to us, and they didn't even know they were doing it."

His avatar. Cerberus was Hades' avatar. It made a horrible kind of sense—Cerberus's fierce loyalty to Hades, the peculiar bond they shared … the fact that Hades had taken no particular steps to protect the Helm. He hadn't needed to, because it wasn't his avatar. Yet Cerberus had all kinds of supernatural protections. Or, at least, he had before he had split into three. He'd been unstoppable, completely unfazed by anything the shadow shapers had thrown at him. "But he's … he's not a *thing*. How can he be an avatar?"

The words were no sooner out of my mouth than I remembered Apollo saying that he thought Athena's avatar was her owl.

"Avatars aren't usually living beings," Adrian said, "because living beings die. But what better avatar for the Lord of the Dead than an undying hellhound that never leaves the protection of his underworld? Or he didn't, anyway, until you got involved and split him into killable pieces."

A pang of guilt pierced me. It was true. Without the protection of his bond with Hades, or of his own natural form, Cerberus had been vulnerable. Look what I had done. In trying to save Hades, I'd destroyed him. Now that the shadow shapers had both the god and his avatar in their power, Hades' hours were numbered.

"Mrs Emery will be here in the morning," Adrian said, "just after sunrise. I'm going to try to get a little shut-eye before then. It's going to be a big day."

"Don't let the bed bugs crawl into your ears and lay eggs in your brain." I could hardly move my mouth to form the words, my brain vomiting out sarcasm on auto-pilot while inside I screamed in protest. How had the shadow shapers known what Hades' avatar was, when even Apollo didn't? And how the hell had I managed to screw everything up this badly?

"I expect to sleep very well. I'll dream of the victory to

come." He let himself out, closing the door quietly behind him.

I stared at it, sick with guilt. The key turned in the lock, and I dropped my head into my hands. In a few hours, the shadow shapers would have the powers of the Lord of the Underworld, and it was all thanks to me.

15

I sat there in a daze, trying to think past the pounding headache and the suffocating guilt. This was a new record, even for me, and I'd had some stuff-ups in my time. In trying to save Hades, I'd done the one thing guaranteed to kill him. My breath came in shallow, panting gasps, and I huddled into my drawn-up knees. His avatar. Cerberus was his goddamn *avatar*, and I'd brought him straight to the enemy. Practically bloody gift-wrapped. It was unbelievable.

Hades would die, and it was my fault as surely as if I'd wielded the knife myself. And Cerberus, too. I sank to the floor and reached out to the nearest dog. I loved the stupid, stick-carrying, slobbering furball.

I stroked his soft black fur. *Wake up, buddy. Please.* I pushed against that strange barrier, but it was as unyielding as ever. I could *see* his essence, right there in front of me, but I couldn't quite reach it. *Please wake up. I'll throw you all the sticks you want. Just come back to me. I need you.*

A tear dropped onto his broad back, soaking into the fur. I pushed harder against those mental barriers, until I could feel my face going red with the effort, and the pressure inside my head became unbearable, as if my brain was about to burst from my ears. None of my struggles made any difference. He was never going to wake up.

I laid my head on his side and sobbed.

A while later, Cerberus had a big damp patch on his back and I felt much better. I didn't cry often, but when I did, it was like a cleansing for my soul. Sitting up, I scrubbed the last of the tears away. Maybe it was a good thing that I looked so broken. If they'd been watching that on their monitors, they'd never suspect I had any fight left in me.

Boy, would they be wrong. We were all still alive and, as long as that lasted, we had a chance. We had an ace up our sleeve with Syl perched on their roof, and I would fight until my last breath to save us all. I could still work with her from my cell and, if all else failed, we could throw ourselves on Apollo's mercy. Perhaps he would find his courage if he realised the shadow shapers now had his uncle's avatar.

So ... I took a deep breath. The crying jag had done nothing for my headache, but I'd just have to push through. *Syl? You still there?*

Yes, she replied immediately. *What happened?*

I didn't want to say it: it made it seem all too real. My mental voice quivered, but it had to be done. *There's good news and bad news.*

Are you okay? Did they hurt you?

Another deep breath. *I'm fine. Let me start with the good news—I know where the key to the collars is. Our old friend Adrian has it in his shirt pocket. And he was going to bed—so all you have to do is find his bedroom and steal it when he's asleep.*

We both knew that wouldn't be as simple as I made it sound, but at least it was somewhere to start.

What about the dog?

For a moment, I thought she was talking about Cerberus, but then I realised she meant the fluffy white yap-yap, Snowy. Adrian had said they'd locked him away. A quick scan of the house confirmed this—I found him curled up on a pile of blankets, fast asleep. I prodded him to open his eyes enough to discover he was in a laundry, and the door was firmly closed. Good. It amused me to think that, in trying to stop me using their dog, they'd actually cleared the way for Syl. Snowy would never have let a cat's entry to his domain go unnoticed.

Out of the picture. They've got him locked up in the laundry.

Okay, what's the bad news?

I sighed. *It's pretty bad. Turns out that Cerberus is Hades' avatar, so they've got Mrs Emery arriving at sunrise, all ready for the sacrifice.*

Shit. That is bad. We're really in trouble.

But they don't know we have Syl, the Secret Weapon, up our sleeves. Are you still on the roof?

Yep. I'm not budging until everyone's gone back to sleep.

Good. Stay there and I'll see if I can find out which room is Adrian's.

I let my awareness spread out through the house, in search of anything I could use. The pickings were pretty slim. The shadow shapers had done a good job of clearing their house of animal life. I found a mosquito on the ceiling of one of the bedrooms, and a moth clinging to the glass doors that opened onto the terrace, attracted by the lights outside.

Things were pretty crook when I was reduced to using mosquitoes, but the insect was actually in a bedroom already, so it was the logical place to start. I nudged the moth further into the house. It would take the little creature a while to make it up to the bedroom level.

I sent the mosquito whining across the room, but it soon became clear there was only a woman in the bed. The door to the room was closed, but I managed to force the insect through the gap between the door and the carpeted floor. Together, we buzzed along the hallway to the next room, keeping down low, hugging the floor. We slipped inside and found two people in the bed. Not sleeping. In fact, very much awake, and rather preoccupied with what was going on under the sheets. The mosquito hovered closer, dancing above their heads.

The man looked up and, before the mosquito or I could react, shot out a big hand. Everything went dark and I was flung abruptly out of the mosquito's head. Probably because it didn't exist anymore.

So much for guys being completely focused on sex.

Back in my cell, the cold of the concrete floor had seeped through my jeans and chilled my butt. I got up and lay down on the bed. Might as well be comfortable while I worked. I closed my eyes and went hunting for the moth.

Lexi? Lucas's mental voice stopped me, hesitant and worried-sounding.

I'm here. Did you talk to Hades?

Yes.

And? What did he say?

You should have seen his face when I told him about Cerberus. He went so white I thought he was going to faint. He said if the shadow shapers find out what Cerberus really is, he's dead. And then he wouldn't talk to me anymore. Do you have any idea what he's talking about?

Yeah, I do. Cerberus is his avatar.

Shit.

Shit is right. But it gets worse—the shadow shapers know it, too.

Lucas swore a blue streak, much more creatively than I would have expected. I'd have to add some of those expressions to my own vocabulary if we made it out of here.

I know, it's bad. Hades is going to kill me, if the shadow shapers don't. But tell him we're working on something. Syl's going to try to get the key to the collar back. If we can just get that damned thing unlocked, our troubles are over. It'll be hello Lord of the Underworld and goodbye shadow shapers.

But how can Syl do that? he asked, his voice laced with worry. *If she can even get it, how's she going to get past the guard down here? He'll kill her.*

I was glad that he was worried for her, but I wished he hadn't brought that up. I was trying hard not to think beyond Step 1, because the rest of the plan was pretty scary. Syl had a predator's natural stealth, and I was reasonably confident she'd be able to nab the key without being caught, but what then? Even if she streaked past the guard and shoved the key under the door of Hades' cell, there'd be a long moment where it was just Syl and a guard with a gun alone in the corridor. She'd be defenceless. It made my heart beat faster just thinking about it.

It's a chance, I said. Maybe the guard wouldn't notice a little black cat sneaking past his door. *The only one we've *got. Tell Hades, so he's prepared. I'll let you know when she's got the key.*

While he spoke to Hades again, I checked on my troops. Syl was still on the roof, and my moth had got distracted in a stairwell, fluttering aimlessly around in the void. Gently, I pushed it back onto course for the upper floor. We had just made it into a long hallway with doors opening off either side when Lucas returned.

I hope I don't have to do that again for a while.

What?

Turn human. His mental voice sounded strained. *Something doesn't feel right.*

An image of how I'd last seen him, hunched over and bleeding, immediately sprang to mind. *Are you still healing?*

No, it's not that. Physically, I'm fine. My human shape just feels ... wrong, somehow. Like it belongs to someone else. I don't know, I'm not explaining it properly. Forget it. Probably just stress.

I sighed and rubbed my aching head. No, it probably had something to do with harbouring a piece of a hellhound's soul. It would most likely cling to the canine form, which was the only one it knew, and resist taking human shape. *I think we're all feeling pretty stressed right now.* Particularly me. Should I tell him what I'd done to him? But I didn't want to scare him, and there was nothing I could do about it right now. *What did Hades say?*

You're not going to believe this. I wouldn't believe it myself, except he doesn't look like the kind of guy to muck around in a situation like this. He paused, as if groping for the best way to phrase what he wanted to say. I got the distinct impression he didn't want to tell me whatever was coming next. *He said to tell you who you really are.*

The bottom dropped out of my stomach and landed somewhere on the floor underneath the bed. *What the hell does that mean?*

Whatever it was, I had a bad feeling that I wasn't going to like it. I hadn't forgotten that fleeting look of guilt on Hades' face that time I'd been telling him and Jake about the weird situation in Newport, where nothing in my home town matched my memories of it. I'd thought, then, that he knew more than he was telling, but I hadn't had a chance since to weasel it out of him.

He said you're not who you think you are. That your whole past is fake, just … just false memories he implanted. He blurted it all out in a rush, as if that was the only way to get through it.

He did what? That's bullshit. Suddenly I was angry, more furious even than I'd been with the shadow shapers. I didn't know what I'd been expecting, but it wasn't that. What the hell? I hadn't even met Hades before I came to Berkley's Bay. Why would he do a thing like that? It didn't make any sense. *That's bullshit,* I said again, my rage boiling down the mental connection towards Lucas.

Lexi, I'm sorry. I'm just telling you what he said.

What possible reason could he have for implanting false memories in my head? And what had he done with the real ones? Had he done this with my consent? Not bloody likely! But how could I prove anything? My memories were all fucking *gone*.

Rage blazed through me, hotter than the fires of the Phlegethon. This was madness. I could never trust him again. How could I believe anything he said to me? What was the point of replacing someone's memories? How did changing Lexi Jardine's past make a difference?

Unless …

Unless I wasn't actually Lexi Jardine. I sat up on the bed, eyes wide open and staring. My heart pounded so hard I thought it might hammer its way out of my chest, and cold sweat broke out all over my body. I covered my mouth with my hands, trying to hold in the scream that was threatening to burst free.

He needed to protect your true identity.

I drew a shaky breath. I wished I was in that room with him, so I could see Hades' treacherous face, to determine for myself what was truth and what was lies. And so I could beat the crap out of the lying bastard. But this was not poor Lucas's fault. I drew a shuddering breath, trying to slow my racing heart. Getting a grip on myself—whoever I was.

So who am I supposed to be, then? I held my breath, waiting for his reply.

He didn't keep me waiting long. *You're Artemis, goddess of the hunt. And he made you human so you could hunt shadow shapers without being captured like the other gods.*

16

Lexi? Are you still there?

Abruptly, I severed my mental connection to Lucas. I couldn't *think* with his words echoing in my head. Artemis, goddess of the hunt. No way. No bloody way. I almost burst out laughing. Me, a goddess?

She was goddess of the moon, too. I stood and paced to the door. I had to move. The sun god was her brother. Zeus's *balls*. Apollo was my brother. Now I really did laugh, banging my head against the door.

Ouch. Not a good idea when my head was already pounding. I bent over, head hanging, leaning my forearms against the door, taking deep breaths. *Easy, now.* Getting hysterical wasn't going to help. But how could this be possible? My mother, my friends—all those people I remembered—they were just a figment of Hades' imagination? No way. No way.

What kind of nightmare had my life become? I turned, and slid down the door to the floor, resting there with my back against the hard wood. My eyes were open, but I no longer saw the bare cell. So many thoughts were clamouring for attention, so many emotions fighting within me: confusion, disbelief, horror.

But most of all, betrayal.

How could Hades have done this to me? My whole past, gone. My life, some kind of ridiculous divine joke. I was Lexi, the Girl Who Didn't Exist. I rested my aching forehead on my drawn-up knees, hugging them to my chest. For the moment, nothing else mattered but the storm raging inside me. I'd thought he was my friend and, all the while, he'd been using me. Deceiving me.

All the doubts I'd felt in Newport came roaring back. If my memories were all false, who was I? What kind of person was I? How much of my life was true, and how much a lie? Were *all* my memories before I'd come to Berkley's Bay now suspect? Maybe none of it was true— maybe my life had begun when I'd woken up in this cell, and everything that I thought had happened before was just a fake memory.

No, that couldn't be right. I had Syl to back me up. We'd been together in Crosston before we'd fled in fear of Anders—surely those memories were real? Unless Hades had screwed with her mind, too … I just didn't know what to believe anymore. Or who to trust. Was Apollo in on this charade, too? Was *Jake*?

An involuntary moan broke from my lips, and I clutched at my head. I would go mad if I didn't stop thinking about it, but how could I think of anything else? I stretched out a leg and touched Cerberus with my foot, just to convince myself I was really awake. His warm solidity confirmed that this wasn't some sick nightmare. If only he were himself. I really needed a hug. Even one of his big, slurpy licks would have helped.

Of course, if he were awake and whole, none of us would be here. Nothing could stand against the hellhound. Why hadn't I ever wondered how it was that I could control such a creature? Stupid. *Stupid.* Shouldn't I have been more suspicious of my strange power over animals? The world had plenty of people with power over the elements, but I was the only one who could control animals—apart from a few shadow shapers who'd stolen that power from the dead goddess Cybele. And I knew I wasn't a shadow shaper. It struck me as odd, now, that I hadn't been more curious. Not until Apollo's ring had started whispering to me had I even started to wonder what my power really was.

I laughed, a sharp, bitter sound. Apollo's ring. Of course I would feel some pull towards its magic if I was his goddamn sister. I felt like such an idiot.

I'm in, Syl said, and her voice in my mind was so

unexpected I jumped. It took longer than it should have to drag my head back into the here and now. I put my hands flat on the cold concrete on either side of me. This was real. This was happening. This rough, hard floor beneath my hands, these sterile white walls, were my prison. Whatever had happened in the past, whoever I really was, none of that changed the fact that I was here, in this cell, and my friends were trapped here, too. Though I wasn't so sure anymore that Hades was a friend.

I stared around the small, bare room. Whatever Hades had done, Cerberus was still my friend. He looked softer, smaller somehow, his indomitable spirit hidden now his glowing eyes were closed. These two still forms stretched out on the floor tugged at my heart with guilt. The shadow shapers didn't know or care about my personal crisis. They were still going to sacrifice this big guy in the morning so they could steal his master's powers. I couldn't afford to sit around feeling sorry for myself. Syl was still working, trying to save us all. I had to help her.

Lexi? You there? Her voice was tinged with panic at my lack of reply. Poor Syl. She wasn't made for this kind of thing, but she was doing it anyway. Hot tears pricked at my eyes. At least I still had her. She was the one piece of my past that Hades couldn't take away from me.

Yeah, I'm here. Sorry, I said. *You're in? That's great. Where are you?*

In some woman's bedroom. Once I got onto her balcony, I turned human long enough to open the door, and now I'm hiding under her bed. Not that I think she would notice unless there was an earthquake. She's snoring louder than a jet engine.

Probably drank too much red wine at dinner. The tight knots of stress loosened a touch as I spoke to my friend. Bantering back and forth across our link like this had the comfort of an old routine, though usually it was me sneaking into danger, not her. She would be the one offering a withering commentary on my sanity.

I can hear someone talking in the next room. I'm going to wait here until it's quiet.

I checked my mental map of the upper floor. Judging from where Syl's life spark glowed above me, she was probably in the first room I'd checked via mosquito-cam earlier. Which meant that the room next door had the amorous couple. I already knew that wasn't Adrian's room. *Good plan. I'll try and find out which one is Adrian's room. Hang tight there.*

My moth had parked itself on a window ledge, resting after many vain attempts to throw itself at the lights it could see outside through the glass. Inside all was dark. I guided it gently back to the job of exploring the bedrooms, creeping under closed doors and checking out the inhabitants.

On the second room, I struck gold. *Found him!* I whispered to Syl. *He's two doors down from where you are now.*

Which direction?

Right as you come out of the doorway. He's in bed. I think he's asleep, but it's hard to tell. My little moth had landed on the bed head, and I sat with it, watching the man in the bed. He wasn't moving, so he could have been sleeping, but he could just as easily have been lying there gloating about the glory to come in the morning.

He was lucky I wasn't actually in the room with him; I could have happily smothered the bastard with his own pillow. Rage seared through my veins, throbbing in time with my heartbeat and the horrible pounding in my head. My life was a lie, and I needed to punish someone. Everyone I'd grown up with—my mother, my brother, my friends—had just died, in a way, wiped away in a single sentence, and my heart was breaking. Maybe they'd never been alive, but they'd felt real to me, despite my limited memories of them. How dared Hades inflict this agony on me? What could be worth this pain?

If my suffering was supposed to save the gods, it obviously wasn't working out according to plan. Was this the end Hades had envisaged, with Cerberus broken and himself about to be sacrificed? How the hell could he have thought this would work?

How the hell did *she* think it could work? I couldn't think of her as me—her motives were as unknowable to me as any stranger's. I had to assume Artemis had been a willing participant in this ridiculous scheme. Surely not even Hades could have done this to his own niece without her consent.

I sure as hell didn't feel like a goddess. I mean, I'd known that humans didn't normally have the kind of power I did over animals, but a goddess? Why had I spent all those months hiding in terror from a bloody fireshaper if I was a goddess? Where were my mighty powers? Look at me, lording it over a stupid moth, bending it to my divine will.

Some goddess.

Could we have a little more certainty than that? Syl sounded on edge. *I don't want to sneak in there and have him jump up and catch me going through his pockets.*

I clenched my fists, clamping down on the urge to yell at her. She was scared, but she was also right to be cautious. Rushing this could jeopardise everything. I wanted to wrap my hands around someone's throat and *squeeze*, but now was not the time to give in to my feelings. I drew a deep breath and forced my fingers to unclench. *Let's give it a little while to be safe.*

I let my head fall back against the door behind me. If I was a goddess, how come the other gods couldn't tell? *He made you human so you could hunt shadow shapers*. Yes, but … even my own brother? Even Apollo couldn't recognise me? He'd said that something about me hadn't felt quite like other humans—Jake had said the same, the first time we'd met—but it obviously didn't feel godlike, whatever it was. I mean, I knew the gods could change form at will, so I was guessing I currently didn't look anything like Artemis, but Apollo and I were twins. Wasn't there something in me that called to him, the way his stupid ring had called to me?

And that was another thing. What had happened to *my* avatar? Where was my power? I searched my brain for a clue, but nothing came. I didn't even know what my avatar was supposed to be. All my memories kept shrieking their insistence on the childhood in Newport, the afternoons spent working at Belmonte's café, giggling with my friend Cath. My brother's bright hair matted with blood as the men carried him away.

But it turned out my brother—my *twin* brother—was very much alive. And though the golden hair was the same, everything else was different. Would he come to rescue us if he knew who I really was? Maybe not. I didn't even know if he liked his sister. I wasn't entirely sure his sister liked *him*. I'd been warming to him lately—he'd been kind of sweet after my meltdown at the Pool of Mnemosyne, and I'd heartily approved of his bloodthirsty attack on the renegade fireshapers. But I'd never been as impressed with him as Syl had seemed to be. Was that some residual memory from Artemis, or Lexi's snap judgement?

I sighed, wondering what time it was. How much longer did we have before dawn and Mrs Emery's arrival? I hauled myself off the cold floor and lay down again on the bed, my chains clinking as I moved. No sense freezing my arse off if I didn't have to.

Once there, I drew in several deep breaths, trying to centre myself. Rage and pain were great motivators, but knowledge was power. I would have to talk to Lucas again. Hades had all the answers, the bastard. I needed to know more.

Lucas? What else did Hades tell you? If I'd been supposed to go hunting shadow shapers, something must have gone wrong. I mean, sure, I'd managed to free Apollo from their clutches, but that had been almost by accident. I hadn't known where he was when I set out for Newport, and rescuing him had been no part of my plan. If Jake hadn't hunted me down and dragged me into his schemes, I would never have gotten involved. That wasn't hunting; that was sheer coincidence.

It explained why Alberto had been so good to me, though. I'd arrived in Berkley's Bay with nothing, and he'd taken me under his wing, given me a home and a job with no questions asked. And here I'd been, thinking what a great guy he was for it, when in reality, he'd been an uncle looking out for his niece.

Not a lot, Lucas said. *He gave me a message for you. Said he hid your divinity deep enough that you could pass for human, but once you change back, there'll be no hiding anymore.*

Once I changed back? Holy shit. Once I changed back, the shadow shapers would be itching to destroy my avatar and steal my power. But first they'd have to get their hands on it. *What's my avatar?*

Your bow.

That made sense, for a goddess of the hunt. Even I knew that Artemis was often depicted with her bow.

I snorted. Even *I* knew? This whole thing was so ridiculous that I'd have laughed if it wasn't my life that was being so completely screwed up. I was Lexi, not Artemis. Human, not a goddess. I felt that, with every bone in my body. Yet I knew that Hades wasn't making this up just to mess with me. Somehow, I was also Artemis. The irony was insane. A couple of weeks ago, I hadn't even believed in the gods. And all the time I'd been one. You couldn't make this shit up if you tried.

Well, at least that's safe, then.

Uh … apparently not. He said he hid it by making it part of you. Your tattoo.

My hand crept to the back of my shoulder, where the small archer decorated my skin. It didn't feel any different to the rest of me. *Seriously?*

Yes. It will re-form when you, um, unleash the inner goddess.

Right. The idea had a certain appeal, if it meant I could use a few shadow shapers for archery practice. *And how do I do that?*

He said you have to say, 'Huntress, awake,' and pull out your bow.

'Huntress, awake'? That's it?

He said it sounds more impressive in Ancient Greek, but apparently my accent is shit so he didn't trust me to pass it on properly in that language. He reckons English will do fine—it's the intention that counts, apparently.

Right. And then I just pull out my bow. I had trouble keeping the incredulity out of my mental tone. Exactly how was I supposed to "pull out" a bow that was currently a tiny tattoo on my skin? *Did he give you any details on how I'm supposed to do that?*

He said you'll know when the time comes.

Great. So helpful, Hades. If I'd rolled my eyes any harder, they would have fallen right out of my head. *Okay. Thanks, I guess.*

Good luck. But Lexi, be careful. If they get a collar on you, we're all dead.

<h1 style="text-align:center">17</h1>

Right. No pressure.

I sent my mind back to my patient moth, still hugging the wall above Adrian's head. Minutes ticked by while I monitored him, minutes where I threw myself into my surveillance so I wouldn't have to think about the rest of this mess. The blinds were drawn, but not all the way. Enough light from the floodlights outside peeked in between the bottom of the blind and the windowsill for the moth to see the room clearly. A desk and chair bulked against one wall, with Adrian's laptop on the otherwise empty surface. A blinking red light showed that he was charging it overnight.

The room had the feel of a hotel room, luxurious but devoid of personality. Small lamps stood on each bedside table. The bed itself was king-sized, but Adrian slept alone. Those crisp white sheets looked cold. The clothes he'd been wearing tonight were draped neatly over an armchair by the window. Hopefully, he'd left the key in his shirt pocket.

The man himself was breathing in a slow, regular rhythm. He hadn't moved the whole time I'd been watching him, so I figured it was safe to send in the troops.

Okay, I said to Syl. *He's asleep now.*

You're sure this time?

Cross my heart and hope to die.

You'd better not, she said darkly. *I'm going to a lot of trouble here to keep your sorry arse alive.*

Okay, bad choice of words. Cross my heart and hope we all get out of here in one piece. Better?

Much. Okay, here I go. Wish me luck.

You'll be fine, Syl. Go get that key. Last I saw it was in his shirt pocket, and that shirt's on the chair by the window. Piece of cake.

I waited with the moth and, sure enough, in a moment, the door eased open soundlessly, and Syl slipped into the room in human form. She closed the door behind her, then stood for a long moment, watching the sleeping man. I could tell she was nervous by the way she hesitated, and I wanted to whisper encouragement, but of course we couldn't communicate while she was in her human shape. All I could do was watch and wait as she screwed up the courage to move away from the door.

The thick carpet swallowed the noise of her footsteps.

She was barely breathing as she glided across the room, and Adrian didn't stir. I watched as she bent over the armchair, her body blocking the line of light coming in underneath the blind. Her hand slid into the breast pocket of the white shirt.

Then she picked the shirt up, turning it over carefully. Her shoulders slumped as she checked the pockets of the black pants beneath it. Shit. Where was the key?

As if she'd heard me, her gaze lifted and roved around the room. The wall opposite the bed was all built-in wardrobes, panelled in dark, gleaming wood. Maybe in there? She drifted across to the desk first, pulling open the single drawer. It made the slightest squeak as it opened, and her flinch was visible from across the room. We both looked at Adrian, but he didn't move.

Bent over, she examined the contents of the desk drawer. Even in her human form, she could call on the night vision of her cat, so the dark recesses of the drawer didn't take long to check out. She straightened again and moved to the bedside table on the far side from where Adrian slept.

That didn't seem likely. If he'd put it in either of the bedside tables, it was probably the one within arm's reach. Sure enough, she came up empty-handed again, and stood for a moment, staring at the large wardrobe doors. Clearly, she was reluctant to tackle them. It would take a while to search every shelf and drawer within, and every minute she spent in this room only added to her danger. She glanced longingly at the door to the hallway and relative safety.

Come on, Syl. You can do this. If only she could hear me. I was afraid she was about to lose her nerve completely. I sent the moth fluttering over to land on the bedside table next to Adrian's head. If the key was anywhere in this room, I reckoned it would be here. Searching the wardrobe would only prolong the agony. She'd have to risk getting up nice and close to the sleeping shadow shaper, in the end. Might as well get it over with.

If the key wasn't in this room, we had a problem, but there was no use borrowing trouble. We'd cross that bridge if we had to.

Syl had tracked the moth's flight, and then she started moving again. For a horrible moment, I thought she was heading for the door, but instead she turned toward the table where the moth waited, though her steps slowed as she drew closer. After an agony of waiting, her fingers closed on the handle of the drawer, and she pulled ever so gently.

Nothing happened. The corresponding drawer on the other side of the room had slid out smoothly. Just our luck that this one appeared to be stuck. She applied more pressure. Still nothing. She glanced uneasily at Adrian, his sleeping face turned towards her. If he opened his eyes, he could hardly fail to see her.

One good, hard tug and the drawer finally opened, with a grating of wood on wood. Syl froze, her eyes wide with fear, trained on the sleeper's face. Adrian sighed and rolled over.

Long moments ticked past. I held the moth immobile, afraid even the faint fluttering of its wings might disrupt Adrian's sleep further. There wasn't a sound in the room except the shadow shaper's breathing. We both listened as it gradually returned to its previous slow regularity.

Still Syl waited. Better to be sure, of course, but she had more patience than I did. I was acutely conscious of the passing of time. This was taking longer than I'd expected, and dawn was creeping ever closer. At last, she let go of the drawer handle and reached inside. There was the faintest sound as something moved inside the drawer, but it wasn't enough to disturb Adrian. She withdrew her hand, fist closed tight around something, and backed slowly away to the door.

Yes! We had the precious key at last. Now all we had to do was get it to Hades. I sent the moth after her, so that when she eased the door open it could flit through into the hallway. She followed it, moving soundlessly, and closed the door behind her. Then she laid the key on the carpet and turned cat between one heartbeat and the next.

Well done! I said, as soon as our link was re-established. Through the moth's eyes I watched the cat carefully pick up the key in its mouth. *Wouldn't that be easier to carry if you stayed human?*

I can carry a bird or a mouse no problem. I don't think a piddly key is going to present any difficulties. And I have better reflexes in this shape.

She was less likely to be noticed, too. *True. Wait here while I check the way ahead is clear.* The moth fluttered down the hallway to the top of the staircase, the only thing moving in the darkness. There were no cameras in here; only outside, which helped. Not that the moth would have caused any alarm, but the cat would. *All clear.*

I don't know how you can do this, Syl muttered as she crept down the corridor after the moth. *I'm so nervous I feel like I'm going to be sick. It's a wonder the smell of my sweat didn't wake him up.*

You did great, I soothed her, scanning the yawning emptiness of the stairwell. Nothing moved, but I wasn't taking any chances. *We'll make a pro of you yet.*

No, thanks. I'm happy to leave the thieving up to you in future.

I'd always prided myself on my abilities—but I wasn't really a thief, was I? A fresh wave of grief hit me. None of that history was true. The only things I could be sure I'd actually stolen were Apollo's ring and the original key to unlock the collars. Oh, and the altarpiece of Manannan Mac Lir I'd swiped from under the mayor's nose. Three measly thefts. My whole identity as this highly skilled ninja of thievery was a lie. I was actually a goddess. Maybe that was why it had never felt wrong to take things from other people. Goddesses were used to getting exactly what they wanted, only nobody called them thieves when they took it.

Syl paused at the top of the stairs. Light from outside flooded through the floor-to-ceiling glass wall of the grand foyer, leaving nowhere for a black cat to hide once she ventured onto the white marble staircase. I forced the moth to land on the railing, though it longed to wing its way toward the bright light and beat itself against the glass. I could probably let it go once Syl reached the darkness of the basement level. We hadn't seen another soul, and there was no reason to think anyone other than the guard in the basement was awake.

What happens now? she asked. *How do I get this key to Hades?*

First step is to get down these stairs, I said. *The night's a-wasting while you stand there waving your tail around.*

I am not waving my tail, she retorted, but she stepped gingerly onto the top step anyway.

The tip of her tail was twitching with nerves, but I could let that slide. This was no time to pick a fight. We were both too tense.

She slipped down the stairs like a silken shadow. We

both breathed a sigh of relief once she'd made it down and found her way into the dark kitchen. A pair of gigantic refrigerators hummed a quiet song side by side, and red numbers glowed above the oven. 4:32. Another hour until dawn? Perhaps a little longer, but not much.

The stairs to the lower level beckoned, lit only by a soft light rising from below—the light from the guard room spilling into the dark hallway. Hugging the wall, Syl started down, her tail still flicking in that nervous twitch.

So, tell me you have some genius plan other than 'sneak past guard and unlock door', she said, her trademark snarkiness less assured than usual. I didn't blame her for being scared. These guys didn't muck around.

In fact, I was scared myself. So much so that I was sitting here stalling, actually contemplating letting her try to sneak past a guard who was on high alert, then stand in the corridor, defenceless, while she waited for Lucas to retrieve the key she'd slipped under the door and unlock Hades' collar. A real friend wouldn't be putting her best friend at risk like that. Not when she had the ability to unleash powers of her own.

I could follow Hades' instructions—as he was obviously expecting me to do—and release the goddess locked away inside me, then blast my way out into the corridor. Who knew what I would be capable of then? Perhaps I could bring the whole house down, destroying every filthy shadow shaper within its walls. I could most certainly manage to hold them off for a moment while we all made our escape, without Syl having to risk herself any further. But I was afraid.

If I turned back into Artemis, what became of Lexi? Would I suddenly become a stranger to my own self? What if I forgot being Lexi completely—forgot my friends, even forgot loving Jake? Sure, I might get my "real" memories back—but how would I know? I couldn't trust myself anymore to be able to tell what was real and what wasn't. The memories I had now certainly felt real enough, and if I lost them, what became of the person they'd belonged to?

Becoming Artemis was a huge step. Once I took it, everything changed, and it wasn't the kind of change I could take back. What if I didn't like what I became? The temptation to turn my back on it all was enormous. I didn't want to be a goddess. I was happy with my own familiar self.

So maybe I should refuse to change and leave getting us out of this mess up to Syl. That could work. I could flutter that damn moth all over the guard's computer screen, long enough to hold his attention while Syl slipped past. It wasn't that much of a risk. And she was prepared to do it.

A simple plan is a good plan, I told her, trying for a light mental tone. I couldn't decide. My heart told me it was too much of a risk. Syl was a delicate little cat, not some big, scary shifter. How could I risk her life? How would I feel if she got hurt because of my cowardice? Like shit, that's how. But still I wavered.

Dammit, Lexi. You can shove your simple plan where the sun don't shine.

It's okay. I'll distract him so you can sneak past.

With your trusty moth? Seriously? That's the plan?

She was right, it was a crap plan. What kind of friend was I, leaving her to do it all alone, when I knew how scared she was? But the alternative was terrifying. What if Lexi disappeared, consumed by the goddess? Artemis would take back her body like a coat that had been worn for a while by someone else, and Lexi would be dead. *I* would be dead, killed by the stranger I used to be.

I jumped up, unable to sit still any longer. Syl was at the bottom of the staircase. I only had a moment more to decide. Whose life would I risk—hers or mine?

Syl, wait, I said, in an agony of indecision. Tears pricked at my eyes. I should say goodbye, in case I was someone else next time I saw her. Would we even be friends? What would a goddess have in common with a cat shifter?

Shouts and the sound of running feet from above startled us both. Syl froze in place at the bottom of the stairs. I hurled myself into the moth's mind. Left to itself, it had begun to flutter at the great glass walls in the foyer, trying to get to the lights outside. Its eyes were suddenly dazzled as someone flicked on the main lights in the foyer, flooding the stairwell. Adrian appeared at the top of the grand marble staircase, calling back along the corridor to another man.

"Where's Nick?" he was yelling. "There's someone in the house."

Shit. He must have woken and seen the bedside drawer that Syl had left open, the empty bedside drawer that should have held the key. He and the other man clattered down the stairs. In a moment, they'd be through the kitchen and down the lower stairs to the basement.

Move, Syl! I urged, diving into her head too. *You're about to have company.*

But my warning came too late. The guard in the room beside Hades' cell heard the commotion and came out into the hallway. He saw Syl as she began to move, and drew his gun.

She streaked across the lounge room at the bottom of the stairs and threw herself behind a treadmill in the adjoining gym. The gun boomed in the enclosed space as he sprinted after her. The clatter of feet on the stairs announced the arrival of Adrian and the other man.

Despite the urgency of the situation, a curious calm descended on me. It was relief, pure and simple, that the decision had been made for me. My choices had all been taken away from me, and now I had to act.

I closed my eyes and whispered, "Huntress, awake."

18

At first, I thought nothing had happened, and my heart stuttered in panic against my ribs. Syl needed me! Then a warm flush swept over my skin, starting from a point on my left shoulder blade.

From my tattoo, in fact.

I reached over my shoulder, fingers seeking that tingling warmth. My skin burned to the touch, and something moved beneath my fingertips. Man, that was freaky. It felt as though something was alive and moving around under my skin.

The thing moved further, wriggling up onto the top of my shoulder where I could see it if I craned my neck just right. It was my tattoo, though now the black lines of the bow glowed a bright silver, and when I blinked, the after image of the bow burned against the inside of my eyelids.

Pull out your bow. I ran my fingers down my arm, and

the tattoo followed them, as if swimming just under my skin. It was the weirdest feeling ever, but I had no time to dwell on it, or think too hard about what was happening. A deadly game of hide and seek was going on in the gym, and I needed to join in before the game finished and Syl lost. I drew the shining tattoo to the back of my hand with a sweep of my fingers.

The bow had always been the largest part of this tattoo, with the archer merely suggested by a few stylised lines. Now it was barely recognisable as a bow, the strong lines condensed into an odd v-shape that arrowed down my middle finger. Golden light burst from my finger tip. I narrowed my eyes against the glare, watching in disbelief as the top of a full-sized bow emerged from my finger.

The physics simply didn't work, but the laws of physics meant nothing where magic was concerned. Somehow, a full-sized weapon was materialising from my finger, drawn from my body by my mere wish. Squinting against the light, I could barely see what was happening, but when the light dimmed, I was holding a bow and a quiver full of golden-fletched arrows in my hands.

Holy shit. Magic was so crazy.

The bow felt right in my hand, the grip smooth, as if I'd held it this way many times before. I slung the quiver across my body, ducking my head in what felt like a practised motion as the strap passed over it. The strap lay between my breasts, already adjusted to the perfect length for the quiver to sit comfortably against my back. I knew my hand would instantly find an arrow when I reached over my shoulder. I felt strong and powerful, and the pounding headache that had plagued me since I woke was completely gone.

And yet, I didn't remember ever using this bow before. I stared at Artemis's bow in my hand, emitting its soft golden light, searching for some kind of memory, anything that tied me to this weapon. There was nothing. Though I held Artemis's bow—though the damn thing had come out of my very body—I was still Lexi. No divine memories had miraculously arrived to fill the gaps in my head. No godly persona had shoved my Lexi-ness aside. I was still me, as lost and confused as ever, only now I was glowing just like the bow.

Outstanding.

Had I done something wrong? Was there some other part of the magic that Hades had forgotten, or that Lucas had omitted to pass on? Surely there must be more to it than this? I had a cool new weapon—yay, me. My body buzzed with energy, but where was the rest of it? Where were my memories, my understanding of my powers and how to use them? Where was my history?

No time now to puzzle it out. Barely an instant had passed, though the whole thing had seemed to take forever.

I could tell Adrian and his companions hadn't yet entered the gym from the sound of their voices, which were too close.

"What are you shooting at, Nick?" Adrian asked, his voice tight with tension. "Who's in there?"

"There was a cat," the voice of the guard replied. "It was just sitting at the bottom of the stairs when I came into the hallway."

"Stinking shifters," Adrian said. "How the hell did they get in? I hate them."

Yeah, well, the feeling was mutual. I was pretty sure Syl wouldn't be inviting him around for dinner any time soon.

You okay, Syl? I asked.

They've got guns. Her voice was tight with barely controlled panic.

Stay out of sight. I'll be there in a second.

What was that gunshot? Lucas's voice sounded nearly as panicked as Syl's had. Something heavy hurled itself against the door of the room opposite mine—a werewolf, no doubt. He would be desperate to get out and join the fight. Wolves had strong protective instincts. *Who are they shooting at?*

"Settle down in there or I'll put a bullet through you," the guard yelled at him. "Get away from the door."

Do as he says, Lucas, I ordered. I wasn't about to tell him it was his girlfriend they'd been firing at. *Don't worry, I've got this.*

Where's Syl? Is she safe?

His concern earned him top boyfriend points, but I had no time to spare for soothing his fears, justified as they were. I was more concerned with that little red spark nestled deep in his consciousness that didn't belong there.

I reeled it in, cradling it within myself, and turned to the slumbering red embers of the other two parts of Cerberus. This time, when I pushed toward them, the barriers that had held me out before melted away. Everything was so easy now. With my eyes shut, I *reached* for those two and drew them back together. Power flowed through me like champagne bubbling in my veins as I shoved the missing part of Cerberus back where it belonged, reuniting the three parts of his soul. They flared a joyous red as they combined. Something within me pulsed in response, and when I opened my eyes, the glow from the bow had ratcheted up another notch.

BOSSY GIRL! Cerberus hauled himself to his feet, tongues lolling from all three mouths. No longer separate, he was back in his familiar monstrous shape, towering over me. I'd never been so glad to see a three-headed dog in my life.

I threw my arms around his neck, narrowly avoiding poking out one of his eyes with the end of the bow. "You're back! Thank God."

There wasn't a mark on him. Just as I'd thought, he'd

been vulnerable split into three. Once I got his essence back together, it was business as usual. *Note to self: Don't let the massive three-headed hellhound split apart in future, no matter how much he pleads.*

He licked me, then sniffed the air. At once, he was on alert, every ear pricked, all his heads staring at the door. *MASTER?*

"Through that door,* I said. "Let's go get him."

Cerberus hurled himself against the door, the chains that had held him parting as if they were no more than thin threads. Being so much bigger than the werewolf, he succeeded where Lucas had failed—on the third blow, the door gave way, disintegrating into kindling under the onslaught. He leapt through the wreckage, greeted by the sound of gunfire.

I had no fear for the hellhound. Now that he was back in his true form, bullets would glance off his supernatural hide just as the centaurs' arrows had done on our memorable trip through the underworld. Sure enough, the guns fell silent, replaced by snarls and screams.

That left the problem of the chain around my own ankle. I gave it an experimental pull, but apparently godhood didn't come with the kind of overpowering strength that being a hellhound did. I had no key, but did

I really need one? Apollo had barged through the locked door of our apartment as if it were open. Maybe godhood came with more subtle power.

"Open!" I commanded the iron around my ankle. Nothing happened.

Hatred bloomed in my heart—hatred for the shadow shapers and their black schemes, hatred for the chain that held me bound when I longed to join the battle in the corridor. I glared at the cuff around my ankle.

The metallic *clink* as it sprang open was the best sound I'd heard in a long time. I shook the thing off and followed Cerberus into the corridor in time to see Adrian fleeing up the stairs. He hurled a gale in his wake that ruffled the hellhound's fur and sent my hair streaming behind me, but I leaned into it and raised my bow. My arrow, propelled by magic, hit him in the back of the leg. He screamed as it pinned him to the stairs, a high, inhuman wail that was cut off as Cerberus bounded up the steps and ripped his throat out.

The giant dog continued up the stairs, where I could hear people calling to each other, and the sound of running feet. Evidence of Cerberus's activities lay strewn along the corridor. The guard lay halfway to the stairs, his blood spattered on the white wall—a dark, ominous red in the dim light. The arm that had fired the gun was no longer attached to his body. It lay a little further along, drenching the surrounding carpet with dark, sticky fluid. Biting off people's arms seemed to be Cerberus's signature move. Unlike Mrs Emery, though, this guy hadn't survived the experience.

Neither had the man who'd accompanied Adrian down the stairs. He lay crumpled at their foot. When I knelt to check his pulse, the carpet squelched beneath my knee. There was no need for arrows; he was already dead. I peered into the darkened gym. *Syl? Where are you?*

Her eyes appeared first, glowing yellow in the dim light from the hallway, then the shape of the little black cat, still holding the key firmly in her mouth.

She followed me back down the short corridor to the door of Hades' cell. *Remind me not to get on Cerberus's bad side,* she said, averting her eyes from the carnage.

That seemed like a good idea. There was a darkness at the heart of my favourite hellhound that was easy to overlook until you saw him in battle. I stared down at the guard he'd felled, the carpet squelching under my feet as I stepped closer. So much blood. Did he have the keys to open Hades' door? The thought of rifling through the dead man's bloodstained pockets turned my stomach.

But I didn't have to, did I? Clearly, it was going to take me a while to get used to this god thing. I kept forgetting I had other means at my disposal now—I could do what I'd done with the chain. Quickly, I took a firm grip on the door handle, directing my fury at it.

It turned, but no sooner had I started pushing the door open than it slammed shut again from the force of a snarling werewolf hitting the other side.

"Easy, Lucas," I said. "It's only me. Let me in."

I pushed again and this time the door opened. The wolf had backed up into the middle of the space, teeth still bared. Hades stood beside him, the dull pewter glint of the magic collar showing at the opening of his shirt. He was otherwise unrestrained. Mundane chains, such as the one that had held me, weren't needed when they had such a way to restrain his powers. He was no threat to anyone without them.

That was something we were about to change. Syl scampered in and dropped the all-important key to the collar at my feet. The werewolf's snarl disappeared at the sight of the little black cat, and he nosed at her, as if checking she were unhurt. In other circumstances, it might have been funny to watch the big werewolf fussing over the tiny cat, who tolerated his attention with as much grace as cats usually showed their admirers—which was to say, not much—but my sense of humour had deserted me for the moment. Seeing Hades made me angry at what he'd done to me all over again.

Lucas shimmered into human form and picked Syl up by the scruff of her neck, his nostrils flaring. She hissed her indignation at being manhandled, though she stopped short of scratching him.

"I smell blood." He glared at me as if it were my fault, Syl dangling from his hand.

"It's not hers."

He continued to frown at me.

"Or mine." I jerked my head in the direction of corridor. "It's theirs."

He put Syl down and pushed past me into the corridor. Hades smiled. "Welcome back, my dear."

To think that I'd once thought Apollo had the most punchable face I'd ever seen. Hades' smugness made me itch to wipe the smile off his face. He looked like a man who'd saved the world singlehandedly and was well satisfied with the way his grand plans had turned out. Well, that made one of us.

"I'm not happy with you," I practically growled at him, scooping the key off the floor. "Turn around."

Surprise flickered on his face before he turned to present the back of the collar to me. I jerked his shirt out of the way and fitted the key into the lock. It turned smoothly and I pulled the two ends of the collar apart.

Hades removed it with a sigh of relief. "That's better." He rolled his shoulders and turned his head from side to side, loosening muscles long-taut with tension.

Lucas backed into the room, a gun in his hand. He must have taken it from one of the fallen; there was a smear of blood on the front of his shirt where he'd obviously wiped it clean on his clothes. His face was pale but grimly determined. "We've got company."

Hades smiled and cracked his knuckles, before stepping past him into the hallway. "Leave it to me."

19

Syl turned human and Lucas immediately moved toward her. But when he would have taken her into his arms, she held him off, examining me with a frown. "Why the hell are you glowing like that? And where'd you get that bow?"

Lucas's gaze swung to me, too, as wary and concerned as hers. Could I damp down the glow? I didn't even know *why* I was glowing—Hades didn't glow, and he was more of a god than I was. I'd seen Apollo light up a couple of times, but I'd always thought that was because he was the sun god, and he seemed to be able to turn it on and off at will. I tried, but it was harder than unlocking doors. Nothing happened when I focused on banishing the soft light.

I gave a mental shrug. We had more important things to worry about. "I'll tell you later. Let's not get left behind." I went after Hades, and they both followed me. Syl's unhappy expression said clearer than words that she knew I was keeping something bad from her.

Hades must have moved fast; there were two new corpses in the hallway, but no sign of the Lord of the Underworld. They lay dead with identical expressions of horror on their faces and not a mark on them. We avoided the gore Cerberus had left as much as possible as we made our way to the staircase. One long dribble of blood on the wall had almost made it to the floor. Syl looked away, pale but determined, as she passed. Adrian lay in a tumbled heap on the stairs, my arrow still protruding from his leg. I bent and yanked it free. It came out surprisingly easily. These were not ordinary arrows, and I didn't want to leave one behind for the shadow shapers. Who knew what power they contained? Certainly not me. I stuck the gory thing back into my quiver, and Syl shuddered. We stepped over Adrian's body and climbed the stairs in search of Hades and his hound.

We entered the empty kitchen, then started up the main staircase to the bedroom level. Snarling from above told us we were headed in the right direction. A gun shot rang out and I quickened my pace, taking the stairs two at a time. By the time we reached the upper level, silence had fallen again.

I held my bow at the ready, an arrow nocked and ready to fly. Fortunately, I recognised Hades in time as he came out of one of the bedrooms, and didn't put an arrow through him.

He raised an eyebrow as I lowered the bow. "Please don't make a pincushion of me."

"I heard gunfire." I said. "Where's Cerberus?"

"He's about somewhere. Don't worry about him—I think our work here is done."

"You mean you killed them all?" Lucas asked, his face pale. As a bouncer, he was probably used to casual violence, but this took it to a whole new level.

"Well, I wasn't going to invite them to afternoon tea," Hades replied caustically. "They are murderers, every one of them, whether it was their hand that held the knife or not. I see no reason to show a mercy they refused to extend themselves."

There must have been a dozen people in the house. He'd made short work of them. I shivered. I'd seen him kill once before, and was quite glad I'd missed the spectacle this time round. There was no mistaking that he was Lord of the Underworld when you saw him in action. He was creepy as hell.

Cerberus trotted down the corridor towards us, his tail held at a jaunty angle, his jaws dripping gore. He was another one whose true nature was easy to forget. He might beg me to throw him sticks, and lick my face endearingly, but he was a hellhound, a pure killing machine. He stopped beside Hades, panting and wagging.

Hades reached up and scratched behind an ear, and the eyes on that head closed in ecstasy. "You're a good boy."

Cerberus nudged his master fondly, making Hades stagger to one side.

"It's a shame Apollo's not here. We could use a good fireball now."

"Why?" asked Lucas. "They're all dead, aren't they?"

"These ones are, yes, but the filth multiply like a plague. There's no reason to leave the rest of them an asset such as this house. This is war. We kill them, we destroy their property, we sow their fields with salt." He bared his teeth in a savage grin quite at odds with the face of the kindly older man he wore. Again, I wondered what he really looked like. Searching my memory—such as it was—provided no clue. I was Artemis and I still knew nothing, goddammit. He gestured towards the stairs. "Shall we?"

We followed him down the stairs and out onto the floodlit terrace. Everything was quiet. The house was far enough from its neighbours that they might not have noticed the gunshots and the screams—they might not even have been home. Many of the homes had seemed unoccupied when we scouted out the area. The tennis court was championship-ready. Beyond the fake green of the court, the natural green of carefully manicured lawn stretched down to the jetty, where the river lapped silently, black in the night. It reminded me horribly of the black waters of the Styx, where Jake was imprisoned. There was no sign now of Mac's boat, or any others, for that matter.

Hades led us onto the grass, eyeing the water thoughtfully. "Even a watershaper would come in handy. We could flood the whole area."

"We met one earlier," Syl volunteered, giving me an anxious look. She knew it was odd that I was so quiet. "A cute guy half-covered in tattoos."

Lucas cocked an eyebrow at her.

"Not that I was looking," she added hastily.

"Oh?" Hades prompted.

She rushed on, trying to fill the silence. "Yeah, he picked us up in his boat earlier. We had some trouble with the local Merrow."

"What kind of tattoos? Did they look Celtic? Knots and such?"

She looked surprised. "Yes. Why? Do you know him?"

"I think I might," he said, and left it at that. Bloody typical. He'd never met a secret yet that he didn't want to keep. He turned his back on the river, then, and contemplated the house. It was huge; three storeys of wealth on display, all glass and steel and concrete. "This should be a safe distance. Let's see what we can do."

A safe distance for what? We stood next to the tennis court, the steps to the first terrace a hundred metres or more away. He lifted his arms, as if he were about to conduct an invisible orchestra. A darkness like smoke issued from his fingertips and coiled about him. Lucas and Syl took a hasty step back, giving him room to work as the black smoke poured forth. It writhed through the air, towards the house.

A groaning sound was the first warning as the black smoke seeped inside through open doors and window cracks. Some of it appeared to sink right through the solid walls as if they weren't there. I could have sworn the house trembled. Then a tile fell from the roof, smashing to pieces on the flagstones of the terrace below. Another followed, and then another in quick succession.

In a rush, the whole roof crumbled, subsiding inwards almost gracefully. The house collapsed in on itself in slow motion, black smoke swirling around it, like vultures circling a dying animal. After the first couple of roof tiles, nothing flew off or crashed to the ground. First the roof disappeared, then the upper windows and balcony doors shattered, leaving great gaping holes for the black smoke to whirl into. Then the balconies themselves disappeared into those black holes, morsels to feed hungry mouths. Bricks toppled inward like dominoes, one after another, an endless rain of bricks peeling away from the walls. With a great crash, the swimming pool suddenly gave way and water poured down the broken walls like tears. The noise was tremendous. The house just kept shrinking, until the walls were only the height of a man, and finally, even that was gone, sunk into a dark hole.

And then, with a great grinding sound, the ground closed up, leaving bare earth and mud and the odd chunk of concrete as the only evidence that there'd ever been a house there.

"What did you *do*?" Lucas breathed.

"I opened a passage to the underworld under the foundations," Hades replied, lowering his arms at last. "Enough to let the house fall through partway … not enough to actually end up with it on my front lawn."

"Wow." The big werewolf shook his head, still dumbfounded. "You are a bad enemy to have."

"Indeed, Mr Kincaid, indeed." With a grinding of rocks, another hole opened in the grass at our feet. Hades smiled around at us. "Shall we?"

Syl regarded the hole nervously. "Not this again! We could call Winston for a ride back to Berkley's Bay instead, you know."

Hades shrugged. "Suit yourself. I'll be going this way, and you're welcome to refresh yourself at my home if you wish."

"I'm coming with you," I said. "Jake's down there."

Hades arched an eyebrow at me. "He is?"

"Oh," Syl said, as if she'd forgotten about him in all the drama.

"You don't have to come," I told her. They'd have to get back to the temple in the heart of Brenvale, but Winston could pick them up from there if they didn't want to brave the underworld.

"No, I'll come," she said. "Just do me a favour."

"What?"

"Don't scream all the way down this time."

20

The plummet down the long dark hole to Hell was just as terrifying as I remembered, but we were soon standing on the flagstones outside Hades' palace. Lucas said nothing, but his eyes were wide as he looked around.

"What I wouldn't give for a nice, hot bath right now," Hades said.

"Jake first," I said.

Hades' brow creased in confusion. "Where is he? Why is he down here?"

"Because that bitch Styx trapped him." Quickly, I explained the circumstances of our bargain with Styx, and how she'd doublecrossed us by wording it in such a way that Jake would never be free to leave her. "Apollo said even he wasn't powerful enough to force her to give Jake up. Only you or Zeus could."

Hades snorted. "It must have nearly killed Apollo to

admit that he wasn't powerful enough for something. But I suppose I should be grateful that you came looking for me, instead of haring off after Zeus. Nice to be considered useful."

I didn't tell him that we'd had quite a dust-up about that, with Apollo all for leaving his uncle to rot while he focused on the search for his father. Our father. Shit. I didn't care anymore; I just wanted Jake freed. We were so close.

Hades cast a longing look at the great doors of his palace. "I imagine you don't want to wait until I've had a chance to clean up?"

"You imagine right. Let's go."

Hades took the path that led to the wharf, where the newly deceased alighted from Charon's ferry to begin their afterlife. The familiar path led us through the mists across the Plains of Asphodel. Cerberus gambolled alongside us, snapping at shredded souls as they drifted past. I'd made this trip several times previously, back before I'd discovered that I wasn't who I thought I was and that Hades had been lying to me the whole time. My current mood was more in tune with the swirling grey mists and less with the sweet white flowers waving among the tall grasses.

Syl and Lucas trailed behind us, hand in hand amongst the flowers, so I walked next to Hades, but there was no easy banter between us as there might have been before. I was still stewing, and I meant to have it out with him just as soon as Jake was free.

Eventually, we reached the wharf and the stony shore of the River Styx. Its dark waters were whipped into peaks by an invisible wind. Soon, no doubt, the ferry would be arriving, and there would be a few familiar faces on board—more shadow shapers who'd learned that it didn't pay to take on the ancient gods. Something stirred within me at the thought: a fierce pride and an anger that went bone-deep, cold and implacable. They would all pay in the end for what they'd done.

"Styx, show yourself," Hades called.

She didn't make her usual instant jack-in-the-box appearance. Maybe she was too busy with Jake. I ground my teeth at the thought, and tried to banish the unwelcome imagery from my mind.

"Will she refuse to come?" Syl asked, after several minutes had passed with no response.

Hades shoved his hands in his pockets; he seemed perfectly relaxed. "The underworld is wide and the river long, so she may be some time, but she won't defy me. I am the Lord of the Underworld and everything in it."

Fine. Must be nice to be so certain of your identity. I settled in to wait, perched on a familiar grey rock. It was here I'd waited impatiently for the ferry all those times, hoping to see Mrs Emery arriving in the afterlife. No such luck, of course. Maybe we should have waited until she arrived before we left the house in Brenvale. We'd missed a chance to finish her off. I'd been so focused on Jake that it hadn't occurred to me until now. Too late, unfortunately. Knowing her, though, she would have somehow got wind of what had happened and never shown up. She was as hard to kill as a cockroach.

Finally, the water swirled, and Styx appeared. Her black gaze swept over us all, lingering on Lucas, before settling on Hades. She smiled, showing her vicious, shark-like teeth. "If I'd known there was a party I would have got dressed up."

Her shoulders were bare except for her black hair. I didn't need to see the rest of her to know she was naked under the ebony water. Black as her soul—if she even had one—the river itself was all the clothing she needed.

Hades sighed. "Styx, I'm tired and cranky and in dire need of a bath. I'm told you have a guest—a young fireshaper. He's a friend of mine and I want him returned."

Styx's face rearranged itself into an expression of butter-wouldn't-t-melt innocence. "Of course, my lord. And so he will be, when our bargain is fulfilled."

"And when will that be, you lying skank?" I burst out. "When Hell freezes over?"

She shot me a filthy look, then attempted to smooth her sharp features into a smile as she turned back to Hades. If that was meant to be ingratiating, there were entirely too many pointy teeth involved to achieve the desired effect. "I don't know what this woman has told you, my lord, but the fireshaper and I made a deal, and he—"

"Styx." Hades didn't raise his voice, but the nymph stopped mid-sentence. "Enough. Fireshaper, now. My bath is calling."

She hesitated, but Hades' *don't mess with me* expression meant business. Her smooth shoulders slumped, and she bowed her head. "Of course, my lord. I'll get him."

"And, Styx." His voice stopped her as she turned away. "I want him unharmed."

She didn't reply, merely sank out of sight, her dark hair fanning out on the surface of the water before slipping soundlessly beneath it. I stared at the ripples where she had disappeared in an agony of impatience. Was he hurt? Would she truly release him? It felt like an eternity before a dark head broke the surface, but this time, it wasn't the hated nymph.

"Jake," I breathed. I felt like a child on her birthday, with the one present she'd longed for finally within reach. He smiled up at me and it was as if the sun had just come out, melting the icy fear around my heart in a hot flush of happiness.

He swam, and then waded, ashore. The black water ran off him like mercury, as if repelled. When he stepped onto the river bank, his clothes were completely dry.

"Are you well?" Hades asked, running an assessing gaze over my favourite fireshaper. He *looked* well. More than well—he looked good enough to eat, in the same dark pants and form-fitting T-shirt he'd been wearing when I'd last seen him. Then, he'd been dying of the curse Styx had placed on him. Now, he looked to be back to full strength. I'd forgotten how tall he was, somehow, and how *alive*. His presence was so compelling I couldn't drag my eyes away. "Somehow I'd expected more of an argument from Styx."

He flashed a quick grin. "Perhaps I didn't live up to expectations. She said I was free to go."

"And so you are," Hades said. "Please accept my apologies for your prolonged captivity." He gazed out across the dark water, but there was no further sign of the nymph. "Styx and I will discuss this more fully later." The look on his face promised that Styx wouldn't enjoy that discussion. I couldn't say that I was heartbroken at the thought.

"Welcome back," Syl said, giving him a hug, and then she drew Lucas forward. "This is Lucas, Joe's brother."

Lucas and Jake shook hands, and then Jake turned to me. "You came back for me."

"Of course," I said, unable to express the joy that was singing in my heart. He looked just as I remembered, only better. More vibrant, more warmth in his eyes when he smiled at me, more laughter in his face. Just *more*. I wanted to hold him tight and never let go. "You promised to take me on a date."

He laughed, and drew me into his arms, turning my face up to his with a hand under my chin. His lips descended on mine and my eyes closed. Surely there was no better feeling in all the world than the gentle pressure of his mouth on mine. I wanted it to go on forever, and I pressed myself against him, urging him to deepen the kiss. I almost dropped my bow on the rocky ground and I didn't care. Happiness bubbled up inside me.

"Far be it from me to interrupt your reunion," Hades said, "but perhaps you could continue it back at the palace, rather than on this draughty riverbank. I know I could do with a bath, and perhaps Jake would like one, too."

"Hell, no." Jake shuddered. "No more water for me!"

Everyone laughed. Jake took my hand in his and we followed Hades back to the palace. I couldn't help sneaking sidelong glances at him. He seemed eager to move away from the black river—and who could blame him?—but not so traumatised by the experience as I'd feared.

"Did she ... treat you all right?" I asked, when he caught me looking at him. I couldn't quite find a way to ask what I really wanted to know. His quip about not living up to her expectations had me intrigued.

He shrugged. "Can't really complain. I'm sure she's bored of chess by now."

"Chess?" Hades cast a curious glance over his shoulder. "That's not how she usually passes the time with her guests."

"She trapped me by insisting on the letter of our agreement—that I was to stay with her until sunrise—rather than the spirit." Jake smiled. "She was particularly unimpressed when I pulled the same trick."

"What do you mean?" Hades asked, as I cast my mind back, trying to remember the exact wording of the bargain.

"I pointed out that she had insinuated plenty, but all I had actually agreed to was spending some 'quality time' with her." His smile broadened. "We played a lot of chess, and I was a most attentive dinner companion, but the magic of the bargain wouldn't let her force me into anything more."

Hades laughed. "Well done. You beat her at her own game."

"She was probably glad to see the back of me. After we'd established that she couldn't get me drunk enough to give in and sleep with her, she pretty much lost interest in having me there."

I smiled up at him, bursting with a fierce pride. She'd got exactly what she deserved, and no more. I was more relieved than I could say; I'd been dreading what kind of damage being the plaything of a dark goddess might have done my bright fireshaper. "That was smart."

"I occasionally have good ideas," he said mildly.

The rest of the walk passed in silence. Now that the excitement was over, I was practically dead on my feet, and I was pretty sure the others were, too, even Hades. Walking with my hand in Jake's through the mists of the underworld felt like a dream, surreal but beautiful, and I was content to live in the moment forever. But before I knew it, the palace loomed out of the mist. Hades must have manipulated the distance in his hurry to get back, because it felt as though no time at all had passed.

The great doors of the palace swung open as Hades trudged up the front steps, though there were no doormen in sight. The servants were all invisible—at least, that was my theory. We trooped into the gigantic foyer after him. The painted eyes of the gods stared down at us from their portraits on the walls. I couldn't help checking out the one of Artemis, with her bow in one hand and the other resting on the head of a hunting dog. She had black hair and serious grey eyes. I couldn't imagine being that person. To be honest, she looked like a judgemental bitch. The only thing we had in common was the colour of our hair.

Hades paused with his foot on the bottom step of the sweeping staircase. "There's not much of the night still remaining, but you are welcome to find yourselves a bed. Or food will be laid out for you if you prefer." He indicated the door to the dining room with a sweep of his hand. "I'm sorry to be a bad host, but I must bid you goodnight."

Syl looked at Lucas. "Sleep sounds good to me."

"Well, bed, at least," he said, with a grin. Werewolves. Too much was never enough.

They headed up the stairs after Hades, and soon Jake and I were alone in the foyer. Hades' family—my family?—glowered down at us from the walls, but I was done thinking about the gods and the mess my life was in. The best thing that had happened to me in a long time was standing right in front of me, and I was ready to carpe the hell out of that diem.

"I can't believe you're back," I said, as he closed the distance between us. I leaned my bow against the wall, then placed my hands flat against his muscled chest, feeling the strong heartbeat there. He was alive and well and *here*. "I missed you."

He covered my hands with his own, then turned one over and placed a kiss in my palm, his eyes never leaving mine. My own heartbeat sped up in response. I could drown in those blue, blue eyes. He kissed the other hand, drawing a small shiver from me. He grinned at my reaction, but I couldn't help it. All my senses were tuned to him.

Still smiling, he released my hands and drew me into his arms. "I missed you, too. I thought about you constantly. I was worried you'd rush off and do something stupid."

"Because I have such a great track record in that department?"

He cupped my face in both hands and stared into my eyes, his expression serious. "Because you are the bravest, most resourceful woman I've ever met, and I knew you would move heaven and earth for me." Then he grinned. "And because you have a terrible track record of doing stupid things and getting yourself into trouble. You need someone sensible to keep an eye on you."

"I'm pretty sure Syl thinks that's her job."

"I had someone else in mind for the role."

I could have reminded him that he was the one who'd gone rushing into a den of shadow shapers trying to rescue Apollo, so he could hardly claim to be all that sensible. But I kind of liked the idea of having him around on a more permanent basis. And I *really* liked the way he was looking at me, as if he were a starving man, and I was the most tempting morsel he'd ever seen. So I let that one slide.

"So, what will it be?" I asked. "Food or sleep?"

"Are they my only two options?" His voice was a throaty growl, and my breath caught in my throat.

And then my stomach rumbled, almost loud enough to shake the paintings down off the walls.

He laughed. "Sounds like food it is, then."

Goddammit. I flushed as he took my hand and led me into the dining room. Was Hades just pulling my leg? If I was

Artemis, wouldn't I be more … I don't know … suave? In control? Surely a real goddess wouldn't have her amorous moments interrupted by her own digestive system. At least I'd stopped glowing once the battle with the shadow shapers was over. That would have been hard to explain away, and I really didn't want to get into the explanations with Jake—at least not until I'd had a few more explanations myself. Hades and I were well overdue for that chat.

A fruit platter, trays of little cakes, plus a selection of cheeses were laid out at one end of the enormous dining table. Tea and coffee were provided in elegant silver pots. It was the perfect supper—nothing too heavy, but enough to satisfy those late-night hunger pangs. My stomach rumbled again at the sight. Some goddess I was. Wasn't I supposed to exist on ambrosia and the prayers of my worshippers or some shit like that?

"The invisible servants strike again," I said, helping myself to some grapes and slices of apple. "How do they always have food ready exactly when it's required?"

Jake poured a cup of coffee and pushed it across to me. "I don't care, as long as they do."

I slowed down after my second cake, and finally noticed that he wasn't eating. I put down my plate and brushed the crumbs off my fingers. "You're not hungry?"

He stood watching me, his arms folded across his broad chest. "Not for food."

Oh, we were back to that again, were we? There was a gleam in his eye that brought the blood rushing to my cheeks—and other parts, too. I stepped into his embrace and wound my arms around his neck. Desire ignited in his eyes as he bent his head. My lips parted, eager to taste him again. His kiss wasn't warm and tender this time, but possessive, almost savage. I pressed myself against the hard planes of his body and gave in to the fire that roared through me at his touch.

"I thought of you constantly," he said. "Only the hope that I might one day escape and see you again kept me going." He nuzzled my neck, then bit it, and desire knifed through me, piercing me to the core. I writhed under his hands as they roamed over my body, a slave to the exquisite sensations they produced. Something bumped against the back of my thighs. I was sprawled on it, my quiver of arrows hastily discarded, before I realised it was the dining table.

"Wait," I gasped. "Stop."

He looked up from where he was trailing kisses down my bare stomach. "Stop?"

I shoved him away, breathing hard. "Jacob Steele, when the invisible servants arrive in an hour or two with the eggs and bacon, they are *not* going to find me spreadeagled on this table."

"I'd eat that breakfast," he growled.

The naked hunger in his eyes almost melted my resolve,

but I stood up and pulled my shirt back down. I was not a teenager. I could wait the two minutes it would take to find a bedroom. Probably.

"Come with me." Grabbing my bow and quiver, I took his hand and dragged him toward the staircase and the bedrooms above. "Breakfast will be served upstairs."

21

I woke next morning to an odd weight on my chest, and a furnace at my back. I opened my eyes on an unfamiliar room. Large windows showed sunlit trees outside. Inside, potted ferns and vases of flowers were dotted around the room on shelves and tables, bright against the soft green walls. I blinked, trying to get my bearings. The weight was Jake's arm, tucked possessively around my body, and the heat that warmed my back was Jake himself, pressed against me as if he never intended to let me go again.

From where I lay, I could see my jeans and bra on the floor. No doubt the rest of my clothes were somewhere around. I was pretty sure we hadn't actually started undressing each other until we got into the room. My bow and quiver leaned against the wall by the door.

That had been … quite a night. Well worth missing a little sleep for. I drew in a deep, satisfied breath, rejoicing in the feel of Jake's skin on mine, the hard length of his body wrapped around me, legs entwined. His breath stirred the hair on my neck. I could stay like this all day. Warm. Protected. Loved.

I closed my eyes again, snuggling a little closer into Jake, expecting to drift off into sleep again. Unfortunately, my brain had other ideas. Now that I was awake, it began obsessing over my change in status, probing the echoing recesses of my memory for any glimpses of my former life. Why hadn't my memories returned with my powers?

It was no use. After ten minutes of this, I was wide awake. Carefully, I wriggled out from under Jake's arm. He murmured a protest, but settled again as I slid out of the bed. In sleep, he looked younger, less careworn, his forehead smooth and expression soft. His long, dark lashes lay on his cheeks, as dark as the stubble on his strong, square jaw. An urge to kiss him awake seized me, but I resisted. He needed his sleep. Instead, I leaned over, my unbound hair trailing over his tanned chest and neck, and dropped a featherlight kiss on his forehead.

After a shower in the white and gold bathroom off our bedroom, I regathered my clothes and got dressed. My stomach rumbled as I laced my boots. I needed food and answers, not necessarily in that order. Hades had better be awake.

Downstairs, I peeked into the dining room, but for

once, the invisible servants let me down. The long table was bare, not a scrap of food in sight. Maybe I needn't have worried about finding a bedroom last night. I grinned. I would never forget that look of raw need on Jake's face as long as I lived.

Well, I thought I wouldn't, but I couldn't really be sure with my memory, could I? My smile faded. Damn Hades. I looked for him in the library, but he wasn't there. I passed the lift to the upper world. Perhaps he'd gone up to the pub. I hesitated, wondering if I should follow him there, but decided to make a proper search of the palace first.

I found him, at last, outside on the terrace, at a sunny table laid with all the breakfast goods I'd expected to see in the dining room. He smiled when he saw me, and waved to the seat on his right.

"Join me? It's a lovely morning for breakfast in the sun."

I pulled out the chair and sat, feeling argumentative. "It's always a lovely morning here. You don't have bad weather in the underworld."

Or any weather, really. It wasn't truly sun, either, but it felt just as good as the real thing. I loaded up a plate with bacon, eggs, and grilled tomatoes and tried to enjoy the warmth on my back. I'd been in such a good mood when I'd woken up, but now my desire to punch something was growing. Hades had better have some damn good answers for me or it might be him.

He watched me shovel bacon until I started to slow, then cleared his throat. "It's good to have you back, Artemis."

I gave him a sharp glance. "Don't call me that. My name is Lexi."

He arched a puzzled brow. "You enjoyed your time as a human?"

I put the knife and fork down, and took a deep breath. "I still am human, as far as I'm concerned. I've got some handy extra powers, but no bloody idea how to use them. And even less idea who the hell I am."

"I don't understand."

Just as well I'd put that knife down. I could happily have driven it right through his hand where it rested on the table. "Oh, *you* don't understand? How do you think *I* feel? I have no memories of my real life, and only fake ones of my pretend life. I'm completely lost here. How could you do this to me? And why in hell did I let you?"

He stared at me in dawning realisation. "You … don't remember your life as Artemis?"

"No."

He rubbed his face, then ran his hand through his grey hair, avoiding my gaze the whole time. "Oh, dear."

"Oh, dear? Is that the best you've got? *Oh, dear?*"

"This wasn't supposed to happen." He looked miserable, but I was in no mood to let him off the hook just because he felt bad.

"No shit. So what *was* supposed to happen?"

"It was your idea. You were beside yourself when Apollo disappeared. Zeus, too, of course, but mainly your brother. You were convinced that there must be a traitor among the gods, so you came to me for help."

"How did I know *you* weren't the traitor?"

For a moment he looked offended, then he sighed. "You really don't remember, do you?"

"That's what I've been telling you."

"You were with me when Zeus's lightning bolt arrived."

"*You* have the other one?" Sneaky bastard—he'd never mentioned it before.

"No. What do you mean?"

"Never mind." I waved a dismissive hand. Right now, I was more interested in the original topic; I could tell him later about our visit to Hestia. "We'll discuss it later. Go on."

"Well, Apollo hared off straight away, looking for Zeus, but then, of course, he never came back. So you wanted to try something sneaky." He smiled fondly at me. "You always were the brainy one. As I said, you thought one of the gods was involved, and there was no way to get close to one without revealing your own godhood, so you asked me to find a way to remove it."

"Remove it?" That sounded remarkably self-sacrificing for a god.

"Well, not remove it, precisely. More to hide it well enough that you would appear human."

"And you succeeded."

"Yes. You suggested somehow severing your bond to your avatar. You really did trust me—you were prepared to let me keep it safe for you. But I came up with something better—a way to hide it deep inside your own body. So deep that your power was hidden."

Maybe not completely. Jake and Apollo had both commented that something seemed odd about me—even Mrs Emery had noticed something strange. But none of them had realised the truth.

"Most gods don't have an avatar the way we do," he continued. "It makes us uniquely vulnerable."

I was momentarily arrested by "most gods". "You mean … there are other gods besides the Greek ones?"

"Of course," he said, as if it should be obvious. I suppose it was; I just hadn't thought about it. Having discovered the Greek gods were real, I should have expected the other pantheons to be, too. "The Celtic ones are the closest to us, in that they have complex tattoos that are related to their power. That's what gave me the idea to hide your avatar in a tattoo, to keep it safe while you were playing human."

"I assure you I wasn't 'playing' human. It felt bloody real."

"Yes. That was the point." He looked away, out across

the lawns to the little bit of bushland behind the palace. "Unfortunately, it worked too well. You were supposed to remember who you really were. I gave you enough false memories for a realistic cover story—"

I broke in. "Whose memories were they?"

"Bits and pieces from a few people," he said. "But most of it was my own invention, based on a house and neighbourhood chosen at random. I never expected you to believe it and actually go to Newport."

It was my turn to look away, as a lump rose in my throat. His deception was my life and all the people I had loved. Just because they had never actually existed, or had belonged to other people, didn't make them feel less real to me. I still mourned their loss.

He shook his head. "But something went wrong. It seems memory is a difficult thing to work with, even for a god. You weren't supposed to forget you were a goddess, even if you couldn't access your powers. You were supposed to stay in touch with me while you searched Crosston for clues to Apollo's disappearance. Instead, you disappeared into Crosston and I lost all track of you. For six months, I worried that you had been taken by the shadow shapers, too, despite all our precautions, and then you suddenly turned up in Berkley's Bay."

"I didn't remember you at all," I said. "And I thought my brother was dead."

"Yes. You had no idea who you really were, and in the end, I decided it was probably safer for you that way. I tried to find Apollo through other means—using the fireshapers, particularly Jake, who I thought was the best of them. All the while, I hoped that your memory would return."

"Why didn't you just tell me?"

"Would you have believed me if I had?"

I shrugged. "Maybe. I don't know."

"I also worried that telling you might damage the magic that was keeping you hidden. Perhaps that was why you'd lost your memory, because it was the only way for the spell to work. If you believed you were a goddess, might it all unravel, and would other gods be able to sense you again? I decided to keep you in the dark until we managed to locate Apollo." He smiled. "In the end, it all worked out for the best. You freed Apollo, even if the path wasn't as straightforward as we'd envisioned."

It all worked out for the best. He poured a cup of tea and I watched him add milk and sugar, with my hands clenched in my lap to hide their furious shaking. My life had been destroyed and he thought that was for the *best?*

"You'll forgive me if I don't feel quite so chirpy about the result as you do," I ground out between gritted teeth. "How do I get my memories back now?" Maybe if I had my real memories back I wouldn't feel so gutted about losing the life I'd thought I had.

He fiddled with the handle of his cup. "I thought they would have come back as soon as you regained your divinity."

"So you don't know how to restore my memory?" My voice was getting shriller. I stared past him at the tree line, blinking furiously. I would *not* cry in front of him. Cerberus emerged from the trees, nose to the ground and tail wagging, as if he'd caught the scent of something. Probably a lost soul. None of them had memories either. "I thought you were the master of the Lethe and the Pool of Mnemosyne. Memory is your *thing*."

"I'm better with dead people," he said gently. "The living are not of my realm."

"You made Tegan and everyone forget they saw you kill Anders in the street."

He sighed. "Making you 'human' was a lot trickier than that. And I didn't actually remove your memories, so I don't know why they haven't reappeared. Perhaps it will take a little time. Try to be patient."

Ha. Patient? Me? And he said he knew me.

"Has your strength returned?" he asked.

"Strength?" I certainly hadn't noticed any more than normal when I'd tried to break that chain. "No, I don't think so." I could get by fine without extra strength. Memories were far more important to me than weightlifting prowess.

Cerberus stood up on his hind legs, resting his front ones against the trunk of a young tree. He pushed, and the sapling fell over. Clearly, there was nothing wrong with *his* strength. All three mouths closed on various bits of the trunk and pulled with enthusiasm.

"You'll have to do something about your dog or you won't have any landscaping left," I said. I was still shaking with rage and emotion. It was time for a change of subject, before I said something I might regret.

Cerberus eventually succeeded in ripping the tree from the ground. He trotted across the lawn toward us with it held in all three mouths, a jaunty swagger to his step.

Hades leaned forward and put his hand on my arm. "If it's any consolation, I'm missing some rather important memories myself. I can't remember anything between talking to Harry about shifts at work and waking up in that cell. I'm sorry about your lost memories, sorrier than I can say. But sometimes, when the reward is great, terrible risks are necessary. At the time, you thought it was worth it— you would have paid any price to save your brother." He smiled. "You always were more adventurous than the rest of us."

I turned to look at him. The fact that he'd lost a couple of days hardly compared to what I'd lost. "Was I?" I certainly didn't feel adventurous now, though Syl might have argued that my taste for risking myself in pursuit of other people's belongings indicated a certain recklessness. "Have I changed?"

He regarded me, head tilted to one side. "In fundamentals, no, I don't think so. Artemis is strong, loyal and resourceful, and I think Lexi is, too, even if she hasn't quite as much confidence in her own abilities." He laughed. "But goddesses rarely suffer from self-doubt."

"Where was my home? Who were my friends?" An awful thought occurred to me. "Did I have a partner?" That could get horribly awkward, because Lexi loved Jake, and there was no room in her heart for anyone else. I couldn't even imagine the kind of person a goddess would love.

"A lover, you mean?" He shrugged. "You'd have to ask Apollo; he'd know. You and he were very tight."

I pulled a face. "Bloody hell. My personality must have changed a lot."

Cerberus arrived on the other side of the balustrade that separated the terrace from the grass and dumped his tree trunk, giving me an expectant look. *THROW STICK.*

I stared into his glowing red eyes. "Really, buddy? A few hours ago, you were ripping people's throats out, and now you want to play fetch? You are one strange dog."

He sat down and thumped his tail against the grass. His head was still level with mine where I sat on the terrace above him. *THROW STICK. NOW.*

"He likes life's simple pleasures," Hades said, smiling

fondly at the hellhound. "Why don't you give it a try? You might surprise yourself."

Considering Cerberus's recent activities, I wasn't sure if Hades was calling playing fetch or ripping people's throats out a "simple pleasure", which was a little disturbing. Sometimes, lately, I felt like the only sane one around, which was saying something, coming from an amnesiac goddess.

I got up and hurdled lightly over the balustrade. Might as well work off some of my frustrations. Cerberus stood, tail wagging enthusiastically, and watched me bend to pick up the tree. I heaved at it so mightily it almost flew straight over my shoulder. My mouth fell open as I stared at Hades, holding the damn tree above my head in one hand as if it really were a mere stick.

"Well, that answers the question of your strength," he said, smiling.

I smiled back, suddenly excited. If my strength was back, did that mean my memories would soon return, too? I turned and hurled the tree almost back to the tree line. Cerberus took off at great speed to retrieve it. I leaned against the balustrade and watched him run, feeling more hopeful.

In no time at all, he was back, red eyes alight with joy, to drop the "stick" at my feet once more. I threw it again.

"He can keep that up all day, you know," Hades said.

I turned to answer him.

Jake stood in the open doorway, a look of shock on his face.

"How did you do that?" he asked in a strangled voice.

Oh, shit. I stared at his ashen face, at a loss for words. This was no way to find out he'd been sleeping with a goddess. I should have told him. My heart began to beat a little faster as I searched for the right way to explain keeping something like this to myself. Why didn't I tell him? The moment lengthened unbearably.

"It's because she's got her divine powers back," Hades said conversationally, stepping in to fill the silence.

I made a horrified shushing motion at him, but it was too late.

Hades looked from one to the other of us. "I'm sorry," he said, showing a rare uncertainty. "I thought you must have told him."

"Told me what?" Jake asked, unnaturally still, as if he was holding himself to the spot by sheer force of will. "What divine powers?"

I did try. I opened my mouth, but I just couldn't force the words out. Couldn't say *I'm Artemis*. My heart pounded against my ribs. The look on Jake's face was frightening, the colour washed out, the spark gone from his beautiful blue eyes. I was still me; this didn't change anything between us.

Hades waited for me to answer, but when it became obvious that I couldn't, he said gently, "She's Artemis."

Jake's eyes widened fractionally, but then the shutters came down over his face, hiding his feelings behind a mask. Only the clenching of his fists betrayed any emotion.

"Sit down and have some breakfast," Hades said, trying to steer the situation back onto a normal footing.

Jake cast a startled glance at the table, as if only just realising there was food laid out. "No, thank you. I'll say goodbye now. I have to get back to Crosston."

Suddenly energised, I hurdled the balcony back onto the terrace, and he flinched at this display of newfound athleticism. "You're leaving already?"

He looked at me, hurt and fury seeping through the cracks in his new armour. "I think that's best, don't you?"

"No!" I started forward, but he stepped smoothly away, leaving my outstretched hand hanging in mid-air. "No, I don't think that's best. Why would I?"

"Because you're a goddess and I'm a mortal," he said, as if that explained everything.

"So? That makes no difference."

"It does to me. It changes everything. I can't believe you tried to keep it from me." He bowed awkwardly to Hades, then turned on his heel and went back inside.

Hades caught my hand when I would have followed him. "Leave it. Give him some time to get used to the idea."

I nodded, but inside I was numb with fear. What if he never did?

<h1 style="text-align:center">22</h1>

A few moments later, I was in the elevator with Hades. Jake had just used it; we had to wait for it to drop back down to the underworld. There was no sign yet of Syl and Lucas. Either they were sleeping late or they were enjoying their time together, just as Jake and I had done a few short hours before. I envied them their uncomplicated relationship. Sure, it might not last forever, but no one was going to tell them that they were too different, that cats and dogs couldn't lie down together. Neither of them would suddenly get cold feet because the other turned out to be different somehow than they'd thought.

My thoughts were bleak as the elevator rose silently. What other bombshells were in store for me? Being Artemis had already screwed up my love life. What about the rest of it? I must have had an established life somewhere that I'd left behind to become Lexi. Where? What did I like? Who did I spend my time with? It was galling not to know. I would have to talk to Apollo about it—and that was galling, too, to be so dependent on someone I barely even liked to find out about myself.

Although, if Hades was to be believed, Artemis had liked Apollo so much she was prepared to give up her divinity for him, at least temporarily. Maybe I'd judged him too quickly. We hadn't exactly met under ideal circumstances. That annoyed me, too. I hated it when other people made snap judgements. It was uncomfortable to feel that I'd done it myself.

I sneaked a quick look at Hades. He was standing facing the doors, apparently lost in thought. I was still dirty with him—so much so that I wondered how our relationship could ever be the same.

He felt my gaze on him and looked at me. "I'm sorry I told Jake, but I assumed you had already done so."

"I meant to," I said, "but I hadn't found the right time."

Was that really true? I knew how devout Jake was in his worship of the gods, particularly Apollo, the patron of fireshapers. Maybe I'd been subconsciously aware that revealing I was the sister of his god was going to be a problem. Not that I would admit that to Hades.

"Better to have it out in the open," Hades said. "He had to know eventually."

"Maybe." I wasn't ready to admit that Hades might be

right about anything. "Or maybe not. I liked being Lexi. I could have stayed Lexi forever, and no one would have had to know any different."

He gave me a sharp look as the elevator doors opened on the red room with the shiny black coffin in the centre. "He would have guessed eventually if you had stayed together. Loving a mortal is hard; they live such short lives, and the pain of moving on through the years without them is great. It's why most of us choose to be alone, or rub along somehow with each other. Only another immortal can truly understand us." We stepped out of the lift and he led the way across the room to the stairs up to the pub. "I spent many happy years with your friend Persephone, and we still get on even though we're no longer married."

Persephone was my friend? I shook my head at the surreal circus my life had become and followed him up the stairs. He paused at the top, with his hand on the door handle, and turned to me. With a shock, I realised that he now wore the face of Alberto, longer and narrower than the face of the older man I associated with "Hades". His grey hair was gone, replaced by the dark, swept-back style of the vampire.

"I envy you in a way," he said. "You have lost so much, yes, but what freedom you have gained. You're free to start again, learn it all again, *live* it all again for the first time. You have, in effect, been reborn. Such an opportunity is given to few people, and is a great gift for us jaded immortals. Make the most of it."

With that, he opened the door and we stepped through into the pub. Not all the lights were on, making the vast room shadowy. The pub didn't open until midday, since Alberto had always said no one had any business drinking before then, so it must be earlier. Someone was whistling in the kitchen and making a lot of banging sounds with plates, so I gathered it must be nearly opening time. Alberto headed towards the kitchen.

And just like that, seeing him back in his familiar surroundings, I was thinking of him as Alberto again. He made such a convincing vampire—must be all the practice he'd had over the years. A shriek of delight came from the kitchen. That sounded like Lisa. Guess she was pretty pleased to see her boss back.

I turned toward the double doors of the pub. There was nothing for me in here. I had things to do, people to see. Plans to make. If I was fast enough, maybe I could even catch a certain stubborn fireshaper before he left town. My footsteps quickened at the thought.

As I opened the inner door, I heard a squeal of brakes, followed by a metallic crunch. Ouch. That sounded expensive. Out of habit, I made sure the inner door was properly closed before opening the outer one.

Sunshine dazzled me. Had I thought the false sun of the

underworld was bright? It had nothing on the real thing. I shaded my eyes and took in the scene before me.

A shiny black four-wheel drive had mounted the kerb in front of the pub and slammed into the bus shelter there. Fortunately, it appeared no one had been waiting for the bus. The bus shelter was warped, its Perspex side wall shattered into pieces that lay all over the monster truck's bonnet. The front of the four-wheel drive wasn't looking too hot either. An ominous hissing from under the crumpled bonnet suggested a damaged radiator. I doubted the car would be drivable, which was a shame, as its shininess suggested it was pretty new.

The driver forced his door open with some effort, and got out. Uh-oh. His ashen face with its neat white beard was all too familiar.

I hurried closer. "Winston! Are you all right?"

"Yes, I think so," he said, but I was no longer paying attention. Now that the car door was open, I could hear a baby crying. I tugged at the back-door handle, but the door wouldn't open. Mireille was in there, strapped into a baby capsule, her little face screwed up in a wail.

Holly kicked the front passenger door open and struggled out past the airbag. Both of them had deployed. That settled it—this car would have to be towed. I pulled again at the back door, but it was wedged shut by the crash.

"Let me," said Jake, pushing me gently aside.

His fingers sank into the door as if it were made of putty rather than metal, and in a moment, he had it open. Holly quickly unbuckled the crying baby and lifted her out, crooning sweet nonsense to her.

"Is she all right?" Winston asked anxiously.

Holly jiggled her soothingly, and the baby's cries began to subside. "She's fine. Just scared by the noise, I think." She walked around to the front of the car to join Winston, and they both inspected the damage gloomily.

"Shit, Joe's going to be devastated," Holly said. Joe's new car! Oh, no.

"I am so sorry," Winston said. "I don't know what happened."

"It's not your fault," she said. "I shouldn't have taken you on the main road so soon. It's only your second lesson."

It was only then that I noticed the L plates on the car. Holly was teaching Winston to drive?

Jake bent down to look at the side of the car. The tyre that had slammed into the kerb and then the bus shelter was flat. A trickle of greenish fluid from the radiator was running into the gutter beneath it.

I crouched beside him. "I'm sorry I didn't tell you earlier. I only just found out myself—I'm still trying to process it."

He stared stonily down at the radiator fluid.

"Please don't go. I haven't changed, not in the ways that matter."

He shook his head, and a pleading note entered my voice.

"I still feel the same way about you. We can make this work."

"You are *Artemis*," he said. "The virgin goddess. Men have been killed just for looking at you. I can't—"

"I'm sorry," I butted in, "did I have sex with someone else last night?" I shook his arm. Why wouldn't he look at me? "You were there—it must have been pretty obvious that I'm no virgin."

"Keep your voice down." He stood up, trying to shake me off, but I stood with him. Winston was still gazing unhappily at the car, oblivious, but Holly was now staring at us intently. Shifter hearing for the win. "That's not the point," he continued. "People like me worship people like you. They don't—they don't shack up with them."

He was already thinking about living together? I didn't know whether to be thrilled or even more frustrated that he was being so difficult about this. "I thought we had something special."

"We did!" He met my eyes at last, and there was nothing but pain in his gaze. "But we can't. We're too different. Don't you see? I can never be more than a fling to you. You've been alive for millennia. I'll be lucky if I live another sixty years. There's no future for us."

"I'll take your sixty years, Jake, I don't care." And I

didn't care who knew it. Even Winston was staring at us now.

He stared down at me, stubborn to the last. "You say that now, but what about when I'm old and bald and all my joints are giving out, and you're still as beautiful as you are now? There's a reason gods and mortals aren't meant to be together, Lexi."

He spoke my name like a caress, and tears started in my eyes. "I don't care, I love you."

There was a long pause. I held my breath, staring into his sad blue eyes. The rest of the world had disappeared; there was only him.

"It's just not right, my lady." He turned and walked away, leaving me to stare at his rigid back.

How come I'd won but I felt like I'd lost? I'd saved Jake from Styx, but still I'd lost him. I'd uncovered the truth about my past, but all it had done was cause me grief. A tear spilled down my cheek, hot against my skin, and I scrubbed it angrily away. If I started to cry now, I might never stop.

Behind me, someone cleared their throat. "Is everything okay?" Holly asked.

I turned back to her, refusing to watch Jake until he was out of sight like some lovelorn teenager. This was *not* going to end here. I refused to give up so easily. "No, but I'll live."

Holly's gaze was full of sympathy. "Oh, honey, he'll

come round, whatever it is." In three quick strides, she crossed to me and gave me a hug, baby and all. "The best bit about fighting is making up."

I sniffed, and wiped away another tear that had managed to sneak out. "Thanks. I hope you're right."

"You know I am. Here, hold Miri for a minute. Babies make everything better."

She handed me the baby, who gazed up at me wonderingly from huge, slate-blue eyes. She smelled like apple shampoo and love, and I laid a kiss on her sweet downy head.

Holly peered into the depths of the hissing radiator, side by side with Winston. They wore identical frowns. "Joe is going to be so mad."

"Don't worry," I said, jiggling the warm bundle in my arms much as her mother had done. It seemed an automatic response to holding a baby. "Apollo will pay."

Winston gave me a panicked look. "Oh, I couldn't ask my lord to pay for my mistake. I will pay for the repairs out of my wages." He scratched his head, looking sadly at the car. "The only thing is, it might take a while to pay off. I hope we can come to some arrangement."

"Apollo will pay," I repeated. He owed me this, at least. I'd saved his life.

In fact, a few people would end up paying before I was done. Some with their lives, but none as much as whoever had caused this whole mess in the first place. Artemis had been convinced there was a traitor among the gods, Hades had said. She'd given up her divine existence to hunt them down. Slumming it as me. But I could continue her work. This shit was personal now. The traitor had screwed with my life, and cost me a future with a man I was starting to think I really couldn't live without.

Just wait until I got my hands on whoever it was. I jiggled the baby, turning over options in my mind. What to do next? How would I find them? They had managed to stay hidden a long time.

First, I would find Zeus. For the first time, it really hit me that he was actually my father. Holy shit. *I had a father.* And man, was it just me, or were the men of this family all useless? My father, my uncle, and my brother had all managed to get themselves caught, or nearly so. Despite this poor judgement, the father of the gods was probably the only one who had the firepower to deal with the traitor. All I had to was work out where to aim him.

But first I had to find him.

THE END

Don't miss the final book in the series, coming soon! For news on its release, plus special deals and other book news, sign up for my newsletter at www.marinafinlayson.com.

Reviews and word of mouth are vital for any author's success. If you enjoyed *Hidden Goddess*, please take a moment to leave a short review where you bought it. Just a few words sharing your thoughts on the book would be extremely helpful in spreading the word to other readers (and this author would be immensely grateful!).

ALSO BY MARINA FINLAYSON

MAGIC'S RETURN SERIES
The Fairytale Curse
The Cauldron's Gift

THE PROVING SERIES
Moonborn
Twiceborn
The Twiceborn Queen
Twiceborn Endgame

SHADOWS OF THE IMMORTALS SERIES
Stolen Magic
Murdered Gods
Rivers of Hell
Hidden Goddess

ACKNOWLEDGEMENTS

Thank you to all my readers who have written to me about this series. It's nice to know you're out there, waiting for Lexi's next adventure! Thanks once again to Mal for beta reading on demand, and to my family for your enthusiasm and support.

ABOUT THE AUTHOR

Marina Finlayson is a reformed wedding organist who now writes fantasy. She is married and shares her Sydney home with three kids, a large collection of dragon statues and one very stupid dog with a death wish.

Her idea of heaven is lying in the bath with a cup of tea and a good book until she goes wrinkly.

9 781925 607000